SEALionaire

Complete Series

A MILITARY ROMANCE

M. S. Parker
Shiloh Walker

Belmonte Publishing, LLC

This book is a work of fiction. The names, characters, places and incidents are products of the writer's imagination or have been used fictitiously and are not to be construed as real. Any resemblance to persons, living or dead, actual events, locales or organizations is entirely coincidental.

Copyright © 2016 Belmonte Publishing LLC & Shiloh Walker Inc

Published by Belmonte Publishing LLC

ISBN-13: 978-1539439578
ISBN-10: 1539439577

SEALIONAIRE BOOK 1

1

Reaper

Standing on the ridge, I stared out into the night.

"Reaper."

I held up a fist, and he lapsed into silence while I continued to recon the desert stretching all around us.

Behind me, the rest of my squad, all members of Seal Team 3, were gathered while we tried to salvage a mission that had been fucked up from the beginning.

Fucked, rushed, and if I ever got my hands on the son of a bitch who had insisted–

Stop! I told myself. Getting pissed about it now wouldn't do me or the squad any good.

"See anything out there?"

I looked over at the lieutenant and shook my head. Big and lean, he ran the show out in the field, and I knew he had to be taking it personally, every last thing that had gone wrong. But if he could stand there and not look like he wanted to rip one of the scraggy little excuses that passed for a tree up from the earth and beat something with it, then I'd hold my temper in too.

He told me once that if I could get my temper under

control, I might one day step into his position. I told him, respectfully, that I'd sooner step into a river full of piranha – bleeding and buck naked with a red target on my dick.

He laughed at me and said he could see my obituary.

Adam Dedman, known to his friends as Reaper, chose death by piranha rather than command. Those who knew him best weren't surprised.

Under all my gear, I was tired, hot, and pissed off, but I managed a level voice as I said, "Nothing but night. Sand."

"Lots of sand." He clapped me on the shoulder and went back to the others while I continued to keep watch.

One recon unit was a little farther out, patrolling. The extraction team was still an hour out, and if we got pinned down, we were fucked.

We might just be fucked anyway. The lieutenant – we all called him Dog, short for Bulldog – had been in contact with command, speaking in low, barely audible tones, but we all knew what he was doing. The extraction point would be almost impossible to reach in an hour.

Especially considering how fucked up things had gotten.

"Aw...fuck..." The last word was rasped out in a low, hoarse cry that was more whisper than scream, and it raised the hair on my arms. I didn't let myself look away though.

That was my friend back there on the ground, getting his tibia set by the medic. Rake broke his leg when our hostage had tried to take off running. Of all the dumb luck. He'd grabbed her and hauled her back just as she was about to fall down into a cave, deep enough to do damage, as evidenced by Rake's injury. She was saved, but he'd crashed down into the dark hole and now the squad was effectively handicapped.

"Easy, Rake." I heard Duke's soft, steady voice, the cadence of the Carolinas heavy in his words as he spoke to his patient. "Okay, buddy. It's done. You with me? Come on, don't pass out on me, you pussy–"

"Fuck off," Rake said, his voice thin.

The retort made all of us smile a little. He was still solid. Rake couldn't use any of the painkillers, not with us being this close to the hot zone and this close to being extracted. We needed to get his leg stabilized and get him back on the move.

A low, whimpering sob rose in the air. "You killed them,"

the woman cried. "You killed all of them."

It was the ninth – no, the tenth time. I was damn tired of it.

"Look, cupcake, it was them or us," Ice growled at her. "And if we died, you were probably next."

Ice, a cold son of a bitch, and while I might not disagree with his statement entirely, he didn't need to antagonize the woman we'd extracted just hours before.

"Ice, why don't you take over?" I called out.

He gave me a lazy smile. "I'd be delighted, Reaper."

We swapped out positions and I settled down on the rock closest to the civilian we'd been sent to rescue, one Kylie Hudson-Wallace. Kylie was pretty much what passed for royalty in America, the daughter of a senator and a former movie star turned philanthropist. She'd been visiting the Middle East on a goodwill mission – or so we'd been told. Personally, I had some doubts and I don't think I was the only one.

She'd been pretty damn cozy with the so-called kidnappers and had started screaming, not just in terror, but in rage when we hauled her butt out of there.

One of them had charged after us, fury in his eyes, and all of them had very real weapons they'd been more than happy to use. They were all dead now, although the group of ten we'd been expecting had been more like thirty. Not bad odds for us, but the entire time we'd been getting shitty intel, and we needed to know why.

"You're going home," I said bluntly, staring at her tear-stained face. Mascara and eye shadow had run to form a messy mask, but she was still beautiful. "Your mother and father are anxious to hear about you. In a few hours, this will all be over."

She stared at me, her lower lip trembling. She opened her mouth, but nothing came out when I lifted my hand and pointed a finger at her.

"You've already reminded us that we killed them. Trust me, I know. That was the job."

Her face transformed into a mask of fury, and she swung out. I caught her hand before she could make contact.

"Don't try that again," I said softly, deadly, meaning every word.

She jerked back, rubbing at her wrist and glaring at me with a look that might have worked on her parents back home.

Over her head, Dog was staring at me. I met his eyes only briefly, but in that look, we both shared an entire, unspoken conversation. Something was seriously fucked up here. The woman gets rescued, and you'd think she'd be happy, nearly gushing with gratitude. Instead, she tried to slap the hell out of me.

2

Reaper

For the rest of my life, I knew I'd remember that night. And her.

Dog.

Rake.

The way those two looked at the rest of us.

The helicopter was hovering overhead. We'd changed the extradition point to a closer location, making getting out even more dicey, and we all knew it. They'd sent down a rig for Rake, and the son of a bitch adamantly insisted that the majority of the team go up first. There was a mad light in his eyes, and we should have seen it, should have done something, but while his leg wouldn't do him shit, nothing was wrong with his hands.

He jerked up the Beretta M-9 and pointed it at his throat. "You boys get safe before you worry about me."

"That's not how this works, Rake," Dog said calmly while the rest of us swore at the dumbass. Like that would do a fucks worth of good.

Rake gave us all a mad little smile. "I had this funny feeling, you know. Like this would be my last dance. But I'll be damned if I let any of you get fucked just because that princess took a run."

The hair on the back of my neck stood on end, and I started toward him.

For the longest time, Rake had insisted he'd die on a mission. I'd always told him he was wrong, that the two of us were going to retire, open up a bar in Chicago, and grow old and ugly together.

His eyes slid my way. "You want me up in that helo, you all go first." His finger tightened on the trigger.

Swallowing hard, I looked at Dog. "He'll pull it."

"I know." Dog nodded and looked at the rest of us, his gaze stopping on Ice. "Get him rigged up. You'll go up right before I do. I'll go up with him."

"You son of a bitch," I said, glaring at him while Ice and Roper escorted the princess over to the ladder that had been dropped down. She was really freaking out now, and I didn't pity either one of them. Ice snarled something at her, and she lapsed into silence. Guess she'd finally picked up on just why he was called Ice.

Duke and Dog were hustling around the gurney, strapping Rake in, getting him ready to lift up once they had him secured. Duke tossed a rig to Dog, and I moved in to help him fit it over his gear, muttering under my breath. "This is crazy." A string of curses followed. "Crazy. Damn it, the skinny bastard doesn't weigh much more than my gear. I'll just strap him to my back and haul his ass up."

Dog chuffed out a laugh. "You might just make it, Reaper."

He punched me lightly before shoving me toward the ladder. "Get on up. It's just the four of us."

I looked over my shoulder and up, saw that Ice had managed to hustle the civilian almost to the top. The wind kicked up from the helo was beating at her hair, tearing at all of our clothes. "Now or never," I said, gritting my teeth.

Giving Rake a quick look, I paused by his feet. "You and I are going to rumble over this, you dumb bastard."

He laughed weakly. "I'll kick your ass any day of the week, pretty boy."

Sneering at him, I gave one more look out and then caught hold of the ladder and started up. It was smooth sailing, one hand over the next. Duke was making good time too and was only a couple yards behind me.

But then...

I sensed more than heard the shouts.

Then the deep concussive boom of ammo echoed through me, bringing all five senses alive.

Looking down, I saw men erupting out of the scraggly cover where we'd just been. Swearing, I went to draw a weapon even as Dog bellowed up at me, his powerful voice carrying over my mic. "Move your ass; that's an order!"

Had to move – they couldn't pull Dog and Rake up while I was there.

Had to move – had to move...

I climbed those last few yards quicker than I'd ever managed before and swung my way into the helicopter, looked down to see Duke right on my ass. We laid down cover fire while the extradition team worked to haul Rake and Dog up.

It was like it happened in slow motion, the bullets that blasted up through the gurney, tearing through Rake.

I was staring into his eyes when they hit, staring into his eyes when he died.

And Dog...agony twisted his face and blood bubbled out of his mouth.

But he kept his eyes on us, even as he lifted his hand.

"No!"

I screamed. Duke screamed. Maybe we all did.

But none of us could stop him from drawing his combat knife and sawing away. We scrambled harder, trying to help the team get them up.

It was a waste of time.

The last I saw of Rake's mutilated body and Dog's pain-bright eyes was right before he made the last, desperate drag of the blade. And over the radio, we all heard his voice. "Go...you...sons of bitches."

His radio kept right on working though.

He died before he even hit the ground, and we listened in grueling, excruciating detail to what those bastards who killed them planned to do. It wouldn't happen because both Dog and Rake's bodies were fucked up beyond all repair. They'd been tortured enough.

Go you, Dog, I thought, dazed.

As the helicopter sped off into the night, I looked over at the woman we'd been sent to rescue.

She was smiling.

3

Reaper

Six Months Later

A BEAUTIFUL BLONDE was curled around me, her hand wrapped around my cock as she moved her head up and down.

The body was willing, but the brain was disengaged. Even when she climbed on top and began to move, nothing other than my dick was interested. She made hungry little noises, and because it wasn't her fault that my mind was a few miles – a few thousand miles – away, I rolled us over and began to drive into her, finding a rhythm that had her moaning, then mewling and finally begging me...*don't stop, don't stop...*

When it was over, I slid away and grabbed my clothes, moving into the shower.

She was lying on her side, smiling at me when I came out.

She wasn't at all bothered to see me sliding my feet into my shoes or grabbing my wallet.

I couldn't even remember her name, although I was sure she knew mine. I knew her type. She hung out at the bars nearest the base and looked for her type – SEALS, generally. I'd seen her before, and for the most part, avoided her. I didn't have anything against her. She wanted a certain rush, the same way I did. I got mine jumping out of planes. She got hers by screwing the men she viewed as badass. No harm, no foul.

"Can I see you again?" she asked.

"No." Shaking my head, I turned to the door. In the mirror, I saw her mouth form a pout, but I knew it was only a display. There was always another man in uniform to take my place.

She'd gotten what she needed from me.

I wish I'd gotten what I needed – a little bit of amnesia.

But I hadn't forgotten a damn thing.

∽

I'D READ the report from cover to cover at least five times now.

I kept hoping it would change, but every single damn word was the same.

Looking up at my commanding officer, I finally placed it face down and got up. I moved over to the far side of the room and stared outside. "Do the others know, sir?"

"They've all been debriefed, yes." Lieutenant Commander Michael Hawkins had a face that could have been carved from granite, and he gave no sign as to the emotions he was feeling. I had a good idea though.

"What will happen to her?"

For a moment, LC Hawkins didn't respond, and I turned to look at him.

"At ease," he said irritably, already reading the expression on my face. "No, she's not getting off. Trust me, Senator Wallace tried damn hard to make it happen, but this was treason. Both Kylie and her mother..."

Treason.

My gut soured, and I thought I might get sick. I moved back to the table and braced my hands on the cold metal, staring down at the report. "Dog and Rake, they died for a traitor."

"They died for their country, doing a job you all believe

in," Hawkins corrected me.

I looked up at him to see if he really believed what he just said, as I heard a knock at the door. Hawkins's dark eyes narrowed a fraction. Officers didn't much like being interrupted. He moved to the door and opened it.

I tuned out the low voices, right up until I heard the visitor say my name.

That tone of voice. I recognized it.

He spoke, and the words connected, in an odd sort of way.

They connected. But they didn't make sense.

They couldn't be real.

"Adam, son...did you hear me?"

4

Reaper

Twelve hours later, I was speeding down I-71, heading toward a hospital in Cincinnati. From Coronado, California to Ohio in the span of hours.

I'd done longer jaunts, but none of them had ever taken as long as this one. It had been interminable, lasting lifetimes.

I kept hearing the voice over and over...

Your mother was in an accident.

Kidney damage, extensive blood loss, collapsed lung. My brain had glossed over almost all of it, but it had latched onto the first – and vital – injury. Mom only had one kidney. If the damage was severe...

I pounded a fist on the steering wheel of the SUV I'd rented and shoved it out of my mind.

My dad had disappeared not long after knocking my mother up. I had no idea who he was, nor did I care. My mom was – and had always been – everything for me. And now she was lying in a hospital bed because of some drunk-ass driver.

Your mother was in an accident.

Navigating the streets with the ease that came from a lifetime of living in the area, I hit the exit ramp going way too fast and hoped there weren't any cops. I couldn't say luck was going my way, but maybe fate decided to take pity on me. No sirens went off as I blasted down the stretch of road going sixty. I laid rubber as I slammed on the brakes, turning into the hospital.

The woman at the front desk took one look at me and tensed.

"Sir, visiting hours—"

"My mother's in ICU. Bad wreck, they don't think she'll make it. Don't even try," I said, striding past her.

One of the security guards stepped between me and the elevators. Fortunately, I knew him. Mom had worked here for twenty years, after all.

"It's okay, Elsie. This is Mary Dedman's boy. He flew all the way here from...where you stationed at now, Adam?"

I didn't want to play the game of Midwestern pleasantries, but Joe could get me up to that room. So I played. "California, sir."

He nodded, then looked at the woman behind the desk. "See? *Chief* Dedman...?" he paused and raised a brow at me.

I nodded again. I'd been promoted to Chief Petty Officer six months ago. Apparently, Mom and Joe were still fond of catching up over coffee.

Mom.

"Chief Dedman's in the Navy, Elsie. He got here as fast as he could."

Elsie frowned but turned back to her desk. "The nurses won't let him in."

Like hell they wouldn't.

∼

MOM WAS AWAKE.

I wanted to think it was a good sign, but that look in her eyes...

When I sat down next to her, she held out a hand, and it was shaking. I folded my fingers around hers, the calluses there rasping against her softer skin. "Mama."

"I knew you'd get here. I could feel it." She closed her eyes, a sigh escaping her. "Adam..."

Lifting her hand to my lips, I kissed it then pressed it to my cheek. "You keep fighting, Mama. You're going to pull through this."

"No, I'm not." She lifted her lashes once more and gazed at me, the pain in her eyes enough to level me. "It's better this way, really. The hurtin' is all over...fast."

She sighed again, and the sound was thick, wet.

"Mom!"

"Hush now. You know there are sick people here..." She managed a weak smile and squeezed my hand. "I love you, Adam."

"I love you too."

Her lids drifted closed over soft blue eyes. "You stay with me now. And, Adam...don't be angry..."

She drifted off to sleep.

"Mama..."

She didn't stir.

Less than an hour later, she was gone.

~

THE WORDS of condolence that came from the medical staff fell on deaf ears.

She held on, waiting for you.

You were able to say goodbye.

I'm sorry for your loss.

I wanted to ask which one – they seemed to be piling up damn high lately.

Rake was gone. Dog was gone. Now Mom.

When they started talking arrangements, all I wanted to do was throw them all out, just lock myself in a room, somewhere dark and quiet. Since it wasn't an option, I just sucked it all in and got through it. The minute there was a lull, I said to nobody in particular. "I have to go."

"Go...?" The nurse closest to me looked confused. Then she nodded. "Of course. You must be exhausted. I know this is all very sudden."

Sudden. Yeah. That covered it. I hadn't seen my mother since Christmas, and now she was gone. All because of some asshole who hadn't been able to say no to a few more drinks.

I was given names, information, told my mother had already made arrangements, and I didn't need to do much. Did I have a phone number?

Of course I had a fucking phone number. What dumbass didn't?

At the look one of them gave me, I realized two things – I'd said that out loud, and they were just trying to figure out where I could be contacted once they were ready to…

"I gotta go." Turning on my heel, I strode for the door. I could handle a world of shit raining down on me, but I couldn't handle the death of my mom. Not right now, not like this. I was almost through the door when the responsibility that Mom had drilled into me made me stop. Without looking over my shoulder, I said, "I'll be staying at her place. Reach me there."

5

Reaper

The bar was a shit hole, the kind that didn't close until the dregs of the night were fading into memory. It wasn't quite miserable enough to suit my mood, but it wasn't the fault of the bar or even the locale. I was in the worst part of Cincinnati I could find, but while the city had some bad areas, it couldn't measure up to the hell holes I'd frequented in my life.

Part of a SEAL's job description was to regularly visit hell holes, and I'd grown accustomed to it.

What I wouldn't give for my phone to ring its ass off right then, alerting me to a mission, but it was quiet. In reality, it was probably a good thing because my head wasn't in a good place.

I wasn't in a good place. I was in the kind of place that could end with people dead, and I'd deliberately avoided going for my phone and trying to find out anything about the man who'd plowed into my mother's car. I already knew too much, thanks to a couple of people at the hospital not being as careful as they should. Two of the hospital staff had been talking, crying. Upset. I got it, really.

But it was dangerous to stand around and drop bombs like

"...the cops on scene mentioned to the paramedics that he'd already been arrested for drunk driving twice."

Twice. He'd been arrested twice. Had he hurt anybody before?

I could find out.

I could find out everything.

I didn't want to do that.

Because if I did that, I'd turn into the kind of man who'd make her ashamed.

"You've had enough, jackass," a woman's tired voice said.

"Listen, you ugly bitch."

The malice in that slurred voice had me lifting my head from the beer I'd been drinking. It was my fourth, but my head was ridiculously clear. Whether it was training or just the fact that they were probably watering down their booze, I had yet to feel even the slightest buzz.

A bald man at the far end of the bar wasn't suffering the same problem. He was so drunk, he couldn't even stand up without bracing himself on the bar. That didn't keep him from making a grab for the rail-thin, scarred woman on the other side.

I took another drink and lowered my glass, setting it down harder than necessary.

The bald dude wasn't alone in his drunkenness. "Bobbi, why don't you just give me and Leo the bottle and mind your own fucking business?" His friend was a piggish-looking man, his nose squashed up below eyes that were narrowed to slits in his fat face.

He caught sight of me looking at him and narrowed those slitted eyes so much that the glint of them was almost impossible to make out. "What the fuck you looking at, pretty boy?"

"That's yet to be determined." I lifted my glass and studied him over the rim before dismissing him, taking another drink of the beer.

He was still looking at me when I put the glass down.

I ignored him and spoke to the woman behind the bar. "Can I get something else?"

She didn't exactly turn her back on the men at the far end, but she edged my way, jerking her chin up. "What you want?"

Pulling my wallet out, I checked the cash. A few twenties. I dropped them all on the surface and smiled at her. "The bottle."

Her lips quirked up a little as she put it down in front of me. "Asking for trouble, pretty boy," she said in a voice too low for them to hear.

Maybe I was.

She moved off after scooping up the cash, tucking most of it into the pocket of jeans so tight it was a wonder she could move. She put one of the bills in the cash register and then smacked the arm of a bum a few seats down from me. "Last call was a few minutes ago," she said. "Get your ass out, Hal."

She hadn't even done a last call, but apparently, the bum realized those words meant something. He more or less oozed over the stool and shuffled out the door. At the same time, Leo glared at Bobbi. "Where the fuck is my drink?" he shouted. He emphasized his demand by slamming his fist down on the bar. It rattled under the blow. Taking the bottle, I lifted it to the light and studied the booze inside. It was some label I'd never heard of, and the smell of it was more akin to turpentine than the Tennessee whiskey it was purported to be.

Bobbi glared at Leo. "Didn't you hear what I said? We had last call, and you're already so drunk you can't see straight. Get your ass out of my place."

"If you don't..." He tried to point at her.

"Why don't you do what the woman says?" I suggested. He still hadn't noticed me holding the whiskey he'd demanded.

His friend was still glaring at me. In fact, he hadn't taken his eyes off me.

A couple of drunk, mean bastards. As Bobbi shot me a look, I glanced at her. "You might want to stay out of the way."

"You might want to make your peace with God," she said. "Leo's a mean son of a bitch."

"Is he?" Smirking, I looked down at them and saw that the drunk piece of shit had finally managed to focus on me. "That makes it even better."

Now that I had both of the men's attention, I upended the bottle. The stink of the cheap alcohol filled the air as it splashed out onto the surface of the bar.

They rushed me.

19

Leo slammed into a chair and fell over his drunk feet before he cleared even a yard.

The pig, though...he was bigger than I realized, and as I'd suspected, all that fat hid a layer of hard muscle. He came at me hard, and I took one punch, welcoming the pain. It cut through the wall of grief inside me, and I wiped the blood from my mouth as I swung my head around to look at him. He had a decent punch, I had to admit.

"That the best you got?"

He swung again.

That one missed by a mile.

Ducking under another wild punch, I caught him in the gut before slamming a hard elbow into the side of his head. Spinning to face his partner, I curled my fingers at him. "Come on."

An ugly smile settled on his lips. I heard the door opening to my left, quiet as it was.

"You are one dumb motherfucker," he said.

It didn't quite cover up the sound of footfalls though. Several of them. Flicking my eyes off to the side, I saw them coming in the mirror over the bar. "Well, hell, man...I guess this'll be more fun than I thought."

6

Olivia

Rubbing my temple with one hand, I put down the tablet and pondered calling in dead.

The problem was, the old man was too shrewd to fall for it. Plus, he paid me really well. Then there was the fact that I kind of adored the guy, and he was going through some seriously shitty days lately. First he'd lost his best friend, then his wife got diagnosed with Parkinson's and then came his own diagnosis, cancer. This latest blow had him looking every single one of his sixty-plus years.

"O?"

At the sound of my shortened name, I looked up. Andi, another one of the boss's strays, had been working for me as my housekeeper for nearly two years now while she went to school to finish up her college degree. She was almost done, which meant I'd soon need to find somebody else to take her place. I hated cleaning. And cooking. And shopping. And I kind of sucked at remembering to check the mail and lock the door and every other thing that didn't involve dealing with the old man.

"What do you need, Andi?" I asked, rising from my desk and grabbing the short, fitted jacket I'd chosen to wear today.

My attire was almost always black and white, though I sometimes mixed it up and went white and black. It worked fairly well with my coloring. Black hair, pale skin, blue eyes. My job wasn't to look pretty anyway. Not that I was dog ugly. I was just...boring. The old man told me I was his secret weapon. Nobody ever expected anything of me because I was so unassuming, and I made sure to dress the part. It made it easier to take care of things.

"Just wanted to make sure you didn't need anything. You've been getting home later and later." She frowned at me from the doorway, tapping a to-go coffee cup in her hand.

My eyes locked on it. "Is that mine?"

"Yes." She smiled slyly. "And you can have it after you drink half of this." She produced a shaker cup – one of those contraptions used for protein shakes, and I groaned. "Oh, don't be a baby. It's got milk and yogurt and strawberries in it. All good things."

"Then why is it in that cup?" Suspicious, I studied her.

"Because it made it easier to shake it all up." Her face was complete innocence.

"Just give me the damn coffee," I whined, exasperated.

"Deal's the deal."

"Fine." Storming over to her, I took the shaker cup and downed half of it in three swallows. It wasn't bad. Gritty but tasty.

When I pointed that out, she said, "A scoop of whey powder too."

"Figures. You're a mother hen, Andi. No wonder you decided to go into nursing." Knowing I probably wouldn't stop until well after lunch – maybe even dinner – I finished the rest of the shake before shoving the cup at her. We traded off, and I held the coffee up to my nose, breathing in the familiar and soothing scent.

"Getting run down and sick won't help him, you know," she said as I turned away.

"Skipping a few meals won't make me sick." I jerked a shoulder in a shrug as I scooped up the tablet and dumped it in my bag. My laptop went in next, keys, phone, charger. That was it. I didn't carry a purse – my license, cash, credit cards all went into a slim case that I kept tucked inside the front pocket of whichever jacket I was wearing. Purses were always in the way, and since I never bothered with make-up or powdering my nose or any of that stuff, why bother carrying another bag?

I was gone in another ten minutes, my driver whisking me away in the ridiculous Philadelphia traffic.

I spent the commute studying the video one more time and then tracking down just what happened to one Adam Dedman.

He'd put four men in the hospital. I'd gotten my hands on a copy of the police report, reading through the cop-talk and trying to find the best way to put some positive spin on this. If I could talk the boss into holding off...

But that wasn't going to happen. I already knew it.

7

Olivia

"So he beat up a couple of drunken lowlifes a few hours after his mother died." The boss put the tablet down and focused on me. "I'm not concerned about this, Olivia."

He was one of the few – the very few – who called me Olivia.

"Sir, the problem is the fallout when you go public." I gave him a smile, leaning forward. "The public eye is about to be on you in a very big way."

My throat tightened at just how much the public eye would be focused on him – and me. And Adam Dedman. Well, there was always the possibility he wouldn't be interested. But that idea was laughable. Really.

"The public eye will look at him and see a grieving man." He jabbed a finger at the tablet. "Especially after they find out his background. A Navy SEAL. I still don't believe it."

Knowing I'd lost the argument, I leaned back and folded my hands in my lap. "I assume you still want me to contact him? Are you certain it's wise so soon after his mother's death?"

"Yes, and you and I are both going." His eyes took on a far off look. "You'll handle him. I just want to attend the funeral.

Keep me in the loop, Olivia."

"Of course." Like I'd do anything else. Keeping the stylus poised over my phone, I asked, "I imagine you'll want to make some sort of gift in acknowledgment of her passing."

He turned away then, moving to stare out over the skyline of the city, the winding ribbon of the Ohio River catching the line of the sun and turning to silver. It was a beautiful view. Up until I'd started working in this position, I'd never seen Cincinnati from this particular angle, but then again, the boss had introduced me to a number of things that were new to me. Stability. A decent, steady job. Friendship. A life.

The boss rarely came into his headquarters these days. The ninety-minute drive was longer than he liked. It was understandable. He was young still, only in his sixties, but he had responsibilities at home that took up more and more of his time.

I lived halfway between his home and the offices on a piece of land he'd given me as a bonus five years ago. I told him it was too much, and he'd brushed it aside. For him, it was a pittance. The man was as rich as Croesus and beyond generous with those he considered most loyal to him.

And he still hadn't answered me.

But I knew he'd heard. Finally, after another moment of silence, he nodded. "Yes, we'll make a donation to the hospital – anonymously. Any ideas on how we should frame the gift?"

Tapping my pen to my lips, I pondered it a moment. The idea, when it came, was simple and perfect. "Make it a scholarship for nurses furthering their education. I imagine the hospital offers some help to those who continue their education like she did. But they often come with strings – agreeing to work for so many years, work so many hours a week. A scholarship would be a nice memorial gift."

"Yes." He nodded, still staring outside. "Make it happen."

A few more moments passed before he came back to the desk. "I understand that my wife's sister is pushing for money again."

"Shocking nobody," I said dryly. There had been a rift between the boss's wife and the sister, one that spanned decades, but the past few months, the sister had become more and more demanding. Cherise Whitney also seemed to think it was time to take certain...actions.

"Should I just make it clear that she's not in the will so there's no point in her pursuing this?"

"That will end with her attempting to rip your hair out by the roots, my girl."

"I bet I'm faster." With a slow smile, I cocked a brow at him, knowing the expression would amuse him.

It did, as evidenced by the laugh. "I bet you are. So we'd end up with a bout of her throwing every possible thing she can find your way. You're my damage control, Olivia. How can you control the damage if you're in the middle of it?"

"I'd just spin a story that your sister-in-law was overcome with grief, and I was willing to be the target of her misplaced anger." I checked my watch. "I imagine you want to attend the viewing. And I have a date with a jailbird."

~

I SPENT the drive researching the most current information I could find on one Adam "Reaper" Dedman. The boss spent it in silence, and our driver didn't attempt to break it. Charlie knew better. Like me, he was another stray the boss had collected over the years, and he understood our employer's moods almost as well as I did.

The silence was welcome. I doubted I'd have much of it once things got rolling.

I had no idea how this was going to be taken or if Adam Dedman would be at *all* receptive. The information I had offered no insight into his personality.

I knew his vital statistics – age, weight, height – things anybody could get if they knew how to do a decent search, along with his address. He'd been in the Navy since the summer after high school, and that was where it started to get harder to find much. He was stationed in Coronado, and there wasn't a lot of information available on him. Up until this morning, there had been no arrests and no trouble with the law, save for speeding tickets that were always paid.

I ended up shutting down the search engine with time left to kill and just studied his most recent picture. He was hot.

There was no other word to describe him. Wide-set eyes that looked like they could cut right through you. High, sharp cheekbones and a jaw that might break a fist if somebody was stupid enough to hit him and unlucky enough to land the punch.

He had broad, heavy-looking shoulders, the kind that made me think he could carry the weight of the world and then some. His short, dark hair left his features unframed, softening him not at all. But there wasn't much of anything about him that was soft.

Except his mouth. I couldn't help but notice that mouth. It was the mouth of a sinner, the kind that would make a saint want all sorts of wicked things.

I was no saint.

I also wasn't in this guy's league.

There was one other detail that I knew about him. I hadn't found it in my research. It had been relayed to me by the boss some years earlier. Reaper was a Navy SEAL. Those guys were all but worshiped by some, and he probably had women coming out of the shadows to kneel at his feet and give him...whatever he wanted. I was a plain Jane through and through, my best features including my brain, my loyalty, and a good pair of legs. I wasn't ugly. I knew what I saw in the mirror though, and nothing could change the fact that I had a square jaw and harsh cheekbones. My mouth was pretty enough, and I had unusual eyes – a gift from either my mother or my father. One of them had given me something nice, at least. But no man would fall in love with me because I had pretty eyes.

The boss had told me once that if I'd dress to complement my strong points, I might surprise myself. But I wasn't looking to surprise myself or impress anybody. I dressed to fit the life I had, the job I had. The simple black suits were easy and professional.

They were also dull and about as likely to catch the eye of the sexy Navy SEAL as the woman wearing them.

Brooding, I tapped my pen against his image.

This wasn't the way I'd envisioned us meeting.

My gut clenched, and I closed my eyes as nerves started to hum, coming to life with a vengeance I hadn't felt in a very long time.

Think about it as a job. Just a job.

8

Reaper

Head against the back of the cell, I stared at the wall.

I had blood on my hands. Literally.

They'd thrown me into a holding cell, which was the third biggest fuck-up of the night – morning. It had been morning, nearly five a.m. by the time the door slammed shut behind me.

Four other guys had been in there, and one of them had decided he didn't like the look of me. I hadn't much liked the look of him either, although by the time I finished rearranging his face, I knew there wasn't much to improve on. Two others had joined in to help him, but they'd regretted it quick enough.

One had gone down like a felled tree when I slammed a fist into his larynx. The other had gotten his head slammed into the concrete floor for his trouble.

When the cops came rushing through, they eyed me, then the one man who had sat out through all of it.

He'd recognized me for military, he told the cops who led me out of the room. He'd served himself, and he didn't see the point in picking a fight for the hell of it. He also stated – loudly – that I'd just finished what they'd started.

I was still in a cell by myself.

"The man you slammed into the concrete has a brain bleed."

I looked up into the impassive face of the cop standing outside the cell.

Cocking a brow, I said, "Maybe he shouldn't have tried to rush me."

"True enough." He nodded, folding his arms across his chest. "You got a visitor."

Grimacing, I shoved myself upright and moved toward the door.

"You going to behave yourself there, big guy?"

"Yes, sir."

He pondered that a moment then nodded at me. "Turn around. Procedure dictates that we cuff you. Hope you understand, Chief Dedman."

"I know all about following procedures." Staring at the opposite wall as he cuffed my wrists through the bars, I brooded over the barrel of the fucking mess I'd thrown myself into. I'd been feeling mean and looking for a fight. I'd found one and then some. And my mother was lying dead in a funeral home. I was supposed to be making arrangements, getting ready to bury her.

My gut twisted and burned. Not just with shame, but with rage directed at myself. I'd dishonored my mother, my rank. What were the chances it was my superior out there, looking to peel some skin off my hide? The guy with the brain bleed...shit, I couldn't feel bad about that. He'd come at my back, and I'd done what I was trained to do. But I wouldn't have been in jail for him to come after if I hadn't been stupid enough – angry enough – to goad a couple of assholes into a fight at some no-name dive.

The cop behind me nudged me aside and opened a door, stepping out of the way so I could enter. Taking one breath to brace myself, I stepped inside.

That bracing breath escaped in a soft sigh as I found myself staring at a complete and total stranger.

A sexy one too, clad in a neat black suit that had probably been selected because it was prim and proper, with a short, fitted jacket and trousers that were equally fitted, making me aware that her ass was top-rate.

Short black hair fell to the middle of her neck. She stood with her back to me, staring out a window not much bigger than a couple of shoeboxes. Strong stubborn shoulders and a long, elegant back tapered down to a narrow waist before flaring out to the kind of hips a man could fill his hands with. Idly, I wondered if her skin was as soft as it looked.

When the door closed, she turned to me.

I almost had to take another breath, because her eyes were...shocking.

Purple-blue. Kind of like some of the flowers my mom liked. *Had* liked...she was gone now. A wave of grief tried to slam into me, but I shoved it down.

Taking a few steps into the room, still holding her gaze, I waited for her to speak.

She didn't.

"I don't recall retaining a lawyer," I said finally.

"Getting a lawyer would be wise." She strode to the desk, moving with an efficiency I found way too appealing. As she sat down, I walked over to the desk and kicked out a chair.

"Shall I ask them to undo your cuffs?"

Cocking a brow, I said, "In the past six hours, I've sent five guys to the hospital. That might not be a wise move on your part."

"Well, I don't plan on picking a fight with you, Chief Dedman." She leaned back in the chair, her lips curving in a quick smile. "Maybe it's me, but I think it's kind of stupid to pick a fight with a Navy SEAL."

Heaving out a sigh, I let my head fall back. "Did Lieutenant Commander Hawkins send you?"

"No." There was a pause, very brief, and in that silence, I heard her take a deep breath. "It wasn't your commander, sir."

That had me straightening, once more staring at her. She met my gaze levelly, but in my periphery, I saw that she was gripping a pen tightly, so tightly that her knuckles pressed sharp against her skin. Those amazing, purple-blue eyes briefly flicked away, and I let my gaze drift down to her mouth. It was soft, almost too soft for her face. The kind of soft that made a man think about kissing her, but that stubborn, strong jaw was almost enough to make a man think twice.

Almost.

Her eyes swung back to mine just as I forced myself to push those thoughts aside. Her lips parted, and she took a deep breath, once more bracing herself.

"Chief Dedman..." She paused, then a faint smile appeared on her lips. "I imagine you've heard this before, but that's an intimidating last name."

"Yeah." I lifted a shoulder. "Mom says it came from her family, way back before they moved over here from England. They were gravediggers. Dead man. One of those trade names like Baker or Farmer."

"Baker or Farmer would be much less intimidating." She was still smiling, and it got me to thinking about kissing her again.

"Yeah, well. You ought to hear what my friends call me."

"Do tell." She arched a brow, a look of expectancy making her eyes even more attractive.

"Reaper." Cocking my head, I waited for her to connect the dots.

"Deadman. The Grim Reaper. Hmm." She nodded and blew out a slow breath. "I guess your friends think it's funny."

"Nah. It just fits. One of them..." I stopped and shook my head, not wanting to think about Dog just then. "Never mind. You aren't here to listen to me ramble. Just what can I do for you, ma'am?"

"Actually, Chief Dedman...or should I call you Reaper? Adam?"

"It doesn't matter. I'm easy." I couldn't stop myself. I glanced at her mouth as I said it, wondering what in the hell was wrong with me. Although for her, all she had to do was say the word, and I'd be damn easy in a heartbeat.

Heat flared in her eyes. She felt it too.

Her voice was cool as she responded. "I think I'll go with Adam. Now, this is going to come as a surprise, but I'm here because..." Under the black jacket of her sensible suit, her strong shoulders tightened. "Your father sent me."

I blinked, waiting for the punchline.

She didn't offer one.

She didn't even blink, not for a good thirty seconds.

"My...father," I said slowly, my hands curling into fists, the short chain between the cuffs rattling as I rose. I moved away from the table and stared at the dull gray stone of the wall in front of me. "You got a name, ma'am?"

"It's Olivia. People usually call me O."

"O, then. You've made a trip to see me for nothing. I don't have a father." Forcing myself to relax, I turned back to her and offered the most relaxed smile I could manage under the circumstances. "It was just my mother and me. Now it's just me."

"You do have a father, Adam." A faint smile flirted with her lips, drawing my attention back to that mouth. The softness of it seemed that much sexier contrasted against the stern lines of her face, like finding out that your straight-laced next door neighbor never bothered wearing panties. "I was a foster child and never knew either parent, but I knew they were out there somewhere."

The insipid *I'm sorry* rose in my throat, but I swallowed it back. I doubted she wanted to hear the words, and they didn't mean anything anyway. It was just something people said to assuage…something. Guilt, maybe. Guilt that some kids had shitty childhoods while others didn't. Empty words always irritated me, and I had the feeling they wouldn't mean much to her either.

"Let me rephrase, O. My father wasn't much more than a sperm donor. He knocked my mother up and then just took off, leaving her alone to handle me by herself. Assuming you have the right Adam Dedman, then I have no desire to hear anything about him, no desire to talk to him or anything else."

"He didn't take off. Your mother asked him to leave." She held up a hand when I opened my mouth to call bullshit on that. "Please…" I snapped my mouth closed, "with your mother's recent passing and your circumstances, other things should take priority. Like getting you out of here."

The door swung open in the middle of that last sentence, and a man I guess you'd call distinguished came inside. Steel-gray, neatly combed hair, a suit a few shades darker, a pleasant smile and bland blue eyes were set in a face that I'd forget within an hour. He came forward, his hand outstretched. He paused, then lowered it once he realized my hands were still cuffed. "Chief Dedman. Gerald Barrett, your lawyer. We'll be leaving shortly for the hearing. I expect they'll ask for a rather high bail, considering the events that took place overnight. I'll push for leniency and should have some luck there, this being your first offense and with your record of service–"

"Hold up." I wanted to tell both of them to back up the train about...oh, hell, two hundred miles. "I don't have a lawyer."

"Don't worry, Chief Dedman. My fees have already been taken care of, and I assure you, I'm the best in the area. Now–"

"I didn't hire you," I said through gritted teeth.

"Your father hired him."

At the sound of O's voice, I slanted a look at her. "My father." I scoffed the words.

I'd gone thirty years without one of those. I'd just as soon keep the status quo.

"Yes." She remained in her seat, one leg crossed over the other, a pen poised in her hand as though she was about to start taking notes. "If you insist on not making use of Mr. Barrett, well, nobody can force you to use his services. But I'm hoping you'll realize that might be...foolish."

Narrowing my eyes at her, I waited.

"How many men have you put in the hospital in the past twenty-four hours?" she asked, her dark head cocked to the side.

"I could have put them in the morgue."

"Your restraint is admirable." She was still waiting for the answer.

"Fine," I said, giving her my back as I turned and looked at the attorney. I'd deal with him for the bail hearing. After that...

9

Reaper

"Out of the question," the prosecutor said after my lawyer – still trying to wrap my brain around that one – requested that I be let out on my own recognizance. "He's sent five men to the hospital in less than twenty-four hours, Your Honor. He's a menace and shouldn't even be considered for bail, at least not without a full psychiatric workup."

I just stared straight ahead.

She'd tossed around more than a few comments about my mental health, but it would take more than that to get a reaction out of me.

Barrett, in his calm and controlled manner, waited until she was done before addressing the judge. "Your Honor, if I may, each of those men came at my client first. I have a signed statement from a witness to the attack in the prison, and he's willing to testify that three men attacked him, and Chief Dedman defended himself. As to the alleged incident at the bar, the bartender has *also* signed a statement that they came at him first. The two men in question – both with a long and colorful history – are refusing to answer any questions. My client states that they came at him after admitting freely that he made some provocative remarks. He just lost his mother, Your Honor. He's a highly decorated member of the United

States Navy. He has no record. This is his first and only offense. I don't see any reason why he can't be released on his own recognizance."

The judge held up a hand when the prosecutor started up again, looking tired.

"The statements?" he asked.

I didn't watch as my lawyer took it up to him, nor did I look over at the judge when I felt his eyes on me.

But when he said my name, respect overruled everything, and I met his eyes. "Yes, sir?"

"You want to tell me what was going through your mind, son?" He waved the piece of paper he'd just finished reading and put it face down. "Not over this. But earlier in the evening. Your...escapades at the bar. I'd like to know just what you were thinking."

"Your Honor," Barrett cut in.

I put a hand on his arm. "I'll answer." Then I met the man's eyes. We'd recognized each other from the time I came in. He'd been in the service himself, I could tell. You get to know each other, even those who'd been living the civilian life as long as this guy had. He was looking for...something. He could either make this easier or harder, but I refused to use a bunch of lawyerly lines and shit to try to make this anything other than what it was.

My fault.

"To be honest, sir, I wasn't."

He arched a brow.

"My mother just died. She's been my rock my whole life. Now she's gone. I haven't had much time to spend with her the past few years and now..." I just shook my head. "So, I wasn't thinking. I was just angry and looking for a fight. Those two boys were looking for somebody to hurt. I presented them with the opportunity to give them what they wanted. They weren't up to the job."

I thought I saw a flicker of a smile in his eyes, but it was gone before it ever fully manifested. "Is that a fact?" He glanced at his folded hands for a moment and then looked up at me. "Son, what do you do in the Navy?"

"Your Honor–"

The judge simply looked over at the prosecutor. She

lapsed back into silence.

When he looked at me, I answered, although not entirely happy about it. "I'm a Navy SEAL, sir."

A few moments later, he made his decision, and the prosecutor shot up from her seat yet again. "Your Honor, this is an outrage. The fact that this man is a Navy SEAL should have no bearing on this case. If anything, that makes his actions more appalling. He's from a class of men who should hold themselves to the highest of moral codes, but he put five men in the hospital."

"Ms. Lincoln, I'm about to hold you in contempt," the tired old judge said, shaking his head. "But, before you have another outburst, let me frame my response this way. The truth is, considering the class of men he's from, while he might have strayed from his code, he didn't entirely fall. If he had, those men would be dead, not just in the hospital. And three wouldn't be there at all if they hadn't attacked him. Now, I would suggest you work out a deal. I have a feeling we won't have this man in our jurisdiction long."

He gave me a quick, commiserating nod, then smacked his gavel down. "Dismissed."

∼

"AND WHAT DOES THAT MEAN?"

The prosecutor practically jumped out of the shadows at us. I'd spent the past hour or so dealing with all the paperwork that came with being processed, and I just wanted out of there.

Olivia and Barrett had been waiting, and, apparently, so had my newest fan. Prosecutor Lincoln.

Olivia shifted subtly forward to cut her off. I couldn't help but smile a little, although the petite prosecuting attorney didn't budge. She kept her attention on Barrett and me. "Do you plan on just disappearing on some mission? I'll subpoena your ass."

"Ms. Lincoln–"

"First off, Miss Lincoln," I drawled, cutting Olivia off. "If I *were* called up, you'd have no chance in hell of issuing a subpoena, unless you think a marshal will have much luck getting into someplace like Syria or Iraq. I think that's a little out of his job description." She tightened her jaw, glaring at me. "They might be used to serving subpoenas to hostile people, but my job takes me *past* hostile. But as to my ass disappearing? More than likely, I'll be facing a military court martial. That ought to suit you just fine. And unlike you idiots out here in the civilian world, *I* won't get a slap on the wrist...like oh, say, the drunk driver who killed my mother or those assholes who jumped me in the bar with their *long* and *colorful* history. I fuck up one time, and I'm done. So...be happy."

The satisfaction that washed over her eyes burned through me like acid. "Well...that being the case...I might be willing to talk about a deal."

"I'm sure you will." I glared at her, filling more disgusted with every passing second. "I'm just quite pleased to know that the boys in the United States military will be the ones dealing with me. Not *you*."

She sneered but turned on her heel and walked away, head high and shoulders back.

"She's really worked up over this, isn't she?"

"Eh, she's new. Trying to climb her way up the ladder." Barrett gave me a kindly smile. "She'll settle down in another year or so and focus on the real criminals."

It didn't help much though.

I still couldn't believe what I'd done.

My phone buzzed at that very moment, and I pulled it out, staring at the message with more than a little dread.

I'd known who it was even before I looked.

Tipping my head back, I stared upward for a long moment. Then I looked at Barrett. "You'll have to figure out what to do next. I need to turn myself over to the nearest military installation."

10

Reaper

"Do you have any idea how many fucking strings I had to pull to get the okay for you to have a few days to get your affairs in order and..." LC Hawkins stopped talking and turned to face me, his weathered face folding into a scowl. "Shit, kid. I know you're down about losing your mom. Losing Dog and Rake the way we did, but you went ape shit on us the past few days. If you hadn't had an exemplary record during your time here, there would be no way in hell you'd be leaving here, except under lock and key, and that would only be for transport to wherever they decided to have your court martial."

"I know, sir." Standing at attention, I stared straight ahead.

Anything he had to say couldn't be any worse than what I'd said to myself over the past few hours. I'd gotten to Wright-Patterson Air Force Base in next to no time, and while I'd been a bit unsettled to see my commanding officer, I wasn't really shocked. My CO was on top of things.

"Just tell me one thing." He planted his hands on his hips and glared. "I get why those idiots in jail got their asses handed to them. But what the fuck were you doing, messing with some low lives in some dive at midnight?"

Running my tongue across my teeth, I debated on that

answer. "Sir, permission to speak freely?"

LC Hawkins waved a dark hand at me.

"Sir, my mother is dead because some piece of shit drunk driver with two offenses on record couldn't wait until he got home to crack open another bottle of Jack." Clenching my jaw, I fought the urge to turn and drive my fist into the nearest wall. It wouldn't do any good and just might do a whole lot of harm. "I was feeling mean and looking for somebody to hurt. A dive offered the best option since I didn't really want to attempt to break into a Cincinnati police station and try to find that said piece of shit and strangle him."

While I was fighting that urge, Hawkins came closer. "You want to tell me how you already know about his past offenses?"

"I didn't break any privacy laws, sir. Two staff members made mention of it. They didn't realize I overheard." I glanced at him as I spoke. And I saw something.

Relief.

Why?

"Sir?"

He opened his mouth, then closed it, turning away to brace his hands on the desk. Big shoulders strained against his uniform as he dropped his head. "Son of a bitch. If I don't tell you..." Finally, he turned and looked at me, his hands locked together behind his back. "He's been arrested before. Went to court once, and the case was thrown out due to a bad warrant."

I saw red.

In my mind's eye, I could see me doing what I should have done. Instead of beating the shit out of some skinny, no-account fool at the bar, I should have found out more about the man who'd killed my mother. Found out everything. I could have been waiting for him when they released him. It might have taken a few weeks, but sooner or later, he'd get released on bail. They'd give him a slap on the wrist and take his license.

Not good enough.

"Whatever you're thinking..."

I looked at Hawkins. "It's not enough."

He blew out a breath and nodded. "Probably not. But we can't carry out justice like that."

"What are you talking about?" An ugly laugh tried to break out, but I fought it. "We do it all the time."

"Not like this. Not for this." He was in my face the next instant. "Don't you go forgetting who you are. I'm trying to take care of this for you. You made one stupid mistake that snowballed. But if I think you're going to get stupid on me, forget having me do you any favors. You'll go to that court martial, you'll do your time, and you'll ask yourself every fucking day what you could have done differently."

Without blinking an eye, I asked, "Don't you think I'm doing that already?"

Hawkins studied me for a long moment and then slowly, he nodded. "Yeah, I imagine you are." He paced over to the window, looking out over the base for a long moment before he spoke again. "I don't know if I'll be able to make this go away entirely, Reaper. I'll try, but things aren't what they used to be. Everybody's bitching about accountability and all that. You know what I mean."

"Yeah." Swallowing the knot in my throat, I nodded. "I know."

I also knew what he was telling me – and what he wasn't.

He'd already mentioned a few things. Nobody wanted to see me do time over this, so chances were, I probably wouldn't.

But I had a bad feeling my career in the Navy was over.

11

Olivia

In the past thirty-six hours, I had placed no less than six calls to Adam Dedman. I knew he was back in Cincinnati. He'd only been gone for roughly seven hours, and when he returned, he contacted Barrett. He'd actually been in contact with Barrett several times.

I knew this because Barrett had been in contact with *me* and had assured me that he'd relayed my requests quite clearly.

Please contact Olivia. She needs to speak with you.

Yet, had he called?

No.

Had he emailed?

No.

He *did* have the email. Barrett had passed it on. Barrett was too efficient *not* to. I knew from personal experience. Barrett had bailed me out of a jam or two back when the boss had first taken me on. And when I'd started cussing the stubborn SOB up one wall and down the other, it had been Barrett who had talked me down.

And I had calmed down. This had to be hard for the guy. But I didn't like being ignored, and I didn't like feeling not coming through for my boss.

Adam Dedman was avoiding me, and that just wouldn't cut it.

The two of us were stuck together whether he liked it or not.

All this avoidance shit was going to stop.

I blew out a breath, compassion softening my heart for a second. I couldn't imagine what he was going through. It had to hurt. If I'd actually known my mother...

But I hadn't.

I'd been found in a dumpster. A dumpster. Talk about abandonment issues. I was less than a day old, and according to the information the boss had eventually been able to dig up on me, my cord was still attached, and I'd been wrapped in newspaper. Not exactly a happy story. There was no telling who my parents were, but one thing was clear – I hadn't been wanted.

More than likely, some high school girl had been left high and dry by her boyfriend. Part of me wanted to say I wasn't bitter. On a good day, I was even able to do just that.

But then I'd remember how miserable my life had been and how I'd dealt with things.

I wouldn't have thrown me away.

And although Adam didn't know it, he'd come from two people who didn't know the concept of throwing something away.

The hard-ass Navy SEAL wasn't going to get away from me so easily. Dodging phone calls, refusing to talk to me...hell. He might have been to hell and back as an adult, but I'd already taken that journey a few times over before I'd even had my first period.

I'd seen him for just a few minutes that morning at the viewing.

I'd kept my distance though. Approaching a man as he stood by his mother's open coffin just wasn't right. Of course, if I'd known he was going to turn around and walk right out, I might have been waiting outside for him.

He was the only family she had. Shouldn't he...I don't know...*be there*? *That* was my kneejerk reaction.

The next reaction was – I wanted to kick myself.

All these trappings with death, they weren't for the one who'd already passed on. They were for the ones left behind, and if Adam didn't want to be there, if he needed to mourn in private, then who was I – or anybody else – to judge him?

I could accept that and understand.

But that son of a bitch needed to talk to me.

Barrett and I had done our best to help him get out of this mess he'd caused for himself, and we needed to get this deal signed before it was suddenly yanked away. I knew enough about LeAnn Lincoln to know how fickle she was. If she decided it would do more for her career to prosecute a Navy SEAL with an impeccable record, then she would.

And since he hadn't returned my calls, I'd just go to him.

One thing the boss had taught me was that sometimes you didn't wait for the other party to make the move. You took the fight to them.

I was in no mood for these power games.

Adam Dedman didn't want to acknowledge his father.

I got it.

I really did.

Nobody understood what it felt like to be abandoned better than me.

But things weren't what he thought, and he'd have to suck it up and move on. The reality he thought he knew was a lot different than the reality that *was*. And *that* reality was still playing out, and he needed to clue into it before everything imploded on us.

The least he could do was hear me out.

I grimaced, even as the thought went through my head.

Maybe he'd hear *me* out.

But would he hear his father out?

That was yet to be determined.

Moving up the sidewalk, I fought the urge to smooth my skirt and brush my hair back. I looked fine when I left the hotel. It was a twenty-minute drive. Nothing disastrous could have happened during those twenty minutes, and I refused to primp.

Of course, the sly voice inside my head was having a field day...s*o why are you wearing a skirt? You* never *wear a skirt.*

Sure I did.

When I wanted to show off my legs.

My legs were my one good attribute, next to my eyes. And my butt.

Okay, so I knew my strong points.

But guys didn't fall for a pretty pair of eyes. They'd notice a nice butt and nice legs.

And I wasn't trying to grab his attention either.

Like hell...

He'd already grabbed mine and some part of me regretted the fact that I wasn't one of those delicate hothouse flowers with perfect breasts and pouty lips with a body to match.

There was nothing delicate about me.

I looked like what I was – a woman who'd grown up fighting for everything she had. Delicate and I had never exchanged a passing glance, and pretty was something I couldn't even hope to achieve. I wasn't going to waste my time trying.

So why was I tugging at my skirt and looking in the reflective panes of the windows to see how my hair looked?

Because I was an idiot.

I started up the steps, only to stop, following an instinct that had never died, no matter how long I'd been off the streets. As I moved down the cobblestone path, I paused, touching my fingers to the flowers that spilled from a basket on the patio. They were so bright and pretty. Somebody had absolutely loved flowers.

I was under no illusion as to who, either.

A noise caught my attention, tugging me toward the back and I continued on.

I followed the little side path around the brick house and came up short. Adam might not be the one who enjoyed the flowers, but apparently, he was no stranger to them. There he was, stripped down to the waist, wearing nothing but a pair of jeans and boots, his hands protected by a heavy duty pair of gloves as he dealt with what looked like some seriously overgrown rose bushes.

Rose bushes. The sight of a man surrounded by scattered rose petals really shouldn't be so attractive, but there you go.

"Are you trying to cut your way to Briar Rose?"

"Go away."

If I had expected to surprise him, I clearly didn't know him very well. He didn't so much as shoot a look in my direction. "You could at least hear me out."

"There's no need. I listened to your messages before I deleted them. You don't have anything I'm interested in." Then he flicked a look at me over his shoulder.

Our eyes met, and heat shot straight through me, coalescing in the pit of my belly. I was forced to clench my hands into a fist – it was either that or move toward him. His eyes went smoldering hot as they swept over me.

"At least nothing that you're offering, sugar." With an indifferent shrug, he focused back on the task at hand. "If he really is my old man, then tell him you tried, and I didn't want to hear it. Relax, sweetheart. You did your job."

"I'm afraid that's not how it works...*sweetheart*." I gave his back a simpering smile. "I didn't do my job. My job is to make sure we minimize the fallout from your little escapade, which, in case you're interested, I'm still trying to do."

He straightened but still didn't look at me. "Trying?"

"Yes, trying. And I'd be succeeding if the DA wouldn't quit being an ass. There's a deal on the table for you, but you need to go in before they decide to trash it. When are you due back in California?"

His shoulder stiffened. It was like somebody had just called him to attention. I wouldn't have been surprised to see him snap off a salute. After a moment, the military posture eased, and he shrugged, causing the wheels in my head to spin.

He'd already been to Wright-Pat. I knew that.

Apparently, his CO had worked a few minor miracles, and he wasn't being forced to head straight to California – *do not pass go, do not collect a court martial...*

Somebody had called in favors.

His mother's funeral was tomorrow. He could at least be here for that. Once he did so, was he ordered to fly out?

I had no idea, but I had to assume the worst.

That meant I had to get him to see the DA first.

"What makes you think I'm going to California? Maybe I'll skip bail and leave the country. Not like Uncle Sam's going to want me anymore." His voice was derisive, and when he shot me a look, I saw all the fury there.

"Don't." No way in hell would I feel sorry for him. It didn't matter that maybe I *wanted* to. It wouldn't help him. "You try to work me, and I'll just walk. Trust me, you're wasting your time. I know your type too well."

Adam scoffed, and I tensed at the mocking sound. "Honey, you don't know anything about my *type*."

"*Honey. Sweetheart...*" I mimicked his growling tone. "Do those really work to keep anybody at a distance? It won't work with me. You're stuck with me until my boss pulls me off, and he's something of a bulldog, Chief Dedman."

His lids flickered. Something flashed across his face – grief, maybe.

Moving past it, I said, "Why don't you just save us the time and shower, come downtown with me so we can deal with all the paperwork?"

"I'm not copping to some deal," he bit off. "If I have to do time, then I do time." He turned back to the roses and began to work, sending more petals and buds fluttering to the ground.

Something inside me softened.

"Do you really think your mother would want you to throw the rest of your life away?"

A pair of short-handed pruning shears flipped end over end and landed in the ground three feet to my right. The handles jutted up, the wicked sharp blades piercing the dirt. Even as I was still staring at the tool, he was stalking toward me, catching me off-guard when he stopped only inches away. He was so close, each individual eyelash was on full display, and when I breathed in, the hot, male scent of him flooded my head.

"You think you got it all figured out, don't you?" he demanded. Sweat gleamed on his skin, beaded in drops to roll down his tempting flesh. Thorns had torn thin jagged lines across his forearms. Probably another way of punishing himself. I wondered if it was a regular thing or if this was only because of the recent tragedy...and everything that happened after.

He loomed over me, his size shadowing the sun, I wasn't a small woman, and the attempt to intimidate me didn't exactly go as planned. Our gazes clashed, locked...held.

I suspected he was used to people backing down when he

glared so fiercely, danger coming off him in waves.

My heart started to race, my blood humming through my system like a river coursing after a hard rain. I swallowed hard and might have backed down – just to get away from the chaos of emotions he was causing inside me. I'd known from the first moment I saw him that he would bring me trouble. One glimpse at his picture was all it took.

A flicker of awareness came and went in his eyes, and as soon as it was gone, I summoned the cockiest smile I had in my arsenal. "Seriously, Adam, if you want to intimidate me, you'll have to do better than that."

"If I wanted to intimidate you, *sweetheart*, I'd be doing a lot more than looking at you." His lids drooped low over his eyes. "And what's the point of that anyway? I just want you to remove yourself from my life. Tell my..." he paused, his lip curling in distaste, "*father*...if that's who he really is, that I just wasn't interested. He couldn't be bothered to hang around when I was growing up, there's no need for him to come around now."

"Are you always this quick to judge?"

"Quick?" A harsh bark of laughter escaped him. "You think nearly thirty years of him *not* being in my life is *quick*?" He laughed again, and the sound was rich...full. I could have lost myself in that sound, rolled in it.

Despite that flicker that had danced between us a few moments earlier, he seemed unaware of it now and continued to talk. Lips curled in a quiver of a sneer, he said, "If he'd shown up in grade school, I would have done backflips. Middle school? It would have meant something. Even high school. But I don't *need* him now. So he can just *fuck off*."

He turned on his heel, a slick military move of dismissal.

Without thinking, I reached out and caught his arm.

Heat arced between us, and I swear I felt it all the way to the soles of my feet.

Immediately, I lowered my hand. Touching him wouldn't be a wise decision. I needed to keep my hands to myself. Especially when he was half naked and hot, his skin gleaming with a fine sheen of sweat.

I was such a sucker for a man who looked like that.

Without thinking, the words spilled out of me. "He was

married. When he and your mother met, he was married. They fell in love. He would have filed for divorce, but your mother wouldn't hear of it. He *wanted* to be involved in your life, Adam. But there were...circumstances."

And my ass was in so much trouble if the boss knew I'd said *any* of this.

For a few seconds, he just stared at me in blank disbelief.

Then fury replaced that blank look, and I almost flinched. "That's *bullshit*," he shouted, shaking his head, his eyes going black. "That's just *bullshit*."

"It's not."

"My mother *never* would have gotten involved with a married man. She *never* would have tried to split two people apart."

Jabbing him in the chest hard enough to skewer him on my nail, I said, "You're not *listening*, big guy. He would have left his wife – for *her*. For *you*. But there were things going on, and your mom said no. She said she couldn't have lived with herself."

He started to argue again, but I cut him off. I understood the male psyche better than some, and when it came to a man like Adam – the testosterone-prone, testosterone *over-laden* male psyche – I understood it a little too much. Giving him an insolent sneer, I said, "I can prove it to you. Unless you're too afraid to see the dirt."

"Afraid?" He practically guffawed. "What's there to be afraid of?"

I lifted a shoulder. "The truth." I held up a hand, stemming the temper that I knew would come sooner or later. "Your mom was a good woman – I know that. But you're painting her a saint and your dad the devil. You're a smart enough man to know that the truth most often lies in the middle ground. Except you won't let yourself see it."

Stony eyes stared at me.

"There were two people trapped in an impossible situation. Give me two hours...and if I don't change how you see things, I'll leave you alone." *I might end up fired, but...*

"Fine." He bit the word off like it tasted bad, but he nodded.

12

Olivia

My boss wasn't just going to fire me; he was going to kill me.

I was hoping my boss understood my rationale. He told me to do whatever it took to convince Adam to give him a chance. To give *everything* a chance.

The house was a ninety-minute drive away. Ninety minutes there, probably thirty minutes on the grounds, ninety back. Three and a half hours. Good thing I'd gone out there early. It was just now coming up on ten. I'd plan for four hours and see if Barrett couldn't finesse things and make it all happen at four. Barrett *would* finesse things – he wasn't one of the most influential lawyers in all of Cincinnati for nothing.

He got back to me within ten minutes, and I could almost feel his genteel, patient tones as he told me he'd worked things out. He'd contacted the DA's office with his request, letting them know it would be quite the favor to the boss if they'd work with Barrett in this case.

Great.

Now I'd have to let the boss know.

But we did what we must.

The prosecutor was young and determined to climb up the

ladder. I understood that, even recognized her drive. She'd be somebody who could either be a best friend, or she'd piss me off. I had no idea which way it would go from here, but if she knew the boss was using his influence, I knew exactly which way *she* would turn.

And none of it mattered, because I had what I needed – a meeting with the prosecutor and Adam Dedman in my car. As we rounded the final curve in the highway, the boss's estate opened up in front of us.

The man at the guard house recognized me and went to wave me through only to stop when he realized I wasn't alone. Although the smile stayed congenial, the flicker in his eyes assured me that everything would change if something set his instincts off.

The two men recognized each other immediately, I realized. Not that they'd ever met. They were both military men. And they recognized the type. The boss only hired former military for security. As the guard took in Adam, Adam was taking him in as well.

"Sousa, this is a guest of mine. Chief Adam Dedman, US Navy. Chief Dedman, this if Lieutenant Sousa, Army. Retired. He did some time with the military police for a while." I arched a brow at Sousa. "Did I forget the terminology or any of your bio?"

"You did good enough, ma'am." He slid his eyes to Adam, taking his measure. "I didn't know you were bringing a guest out today."

"I didn't know I was required to inform you of my every visit."

"Point taken." His pale blue eyes returned to mine. I didn't have to inform him of jackshit. This had been my home for almost a decade, and I still felt more at home here than anywhere else. Sousa knew that.

But Sousa's job was to protect this place – and the boss. He didn't take that job lightly and wanted a heads up next time.

I might have considered it, but Sousa would have given the *boss* a heads up too, and I didn't want him trying to stop me.

Besides, it wasn't like this would happen again.

It would either work or it wouldn't, but repeats would be very unnecessary.

A few more seconds passed, then Sousa retreated back into the guardhouse and pushed a button to let us pass through.

"Damn, and here I thought they kept all the gold in Fort Knox a few hours south of here," Adam drawled, his voice heavily underscored with sarcasm.

When I didn't respond, he continued, "Am I meeting a prince? Is my dad a king of some tiny little European municipality?"

"Would you shut up?"

"If I do that, I don't get to hear your smart ass remarks, O."

The way he said my shortened name was downright pornographic, dirty. Practically orgasmic. In self defense, I blurted out a question that had been eating at me all day. "Why didn't you stay at your mother's visitation?"

He shut down.

It was such a hard and cold switch, I wanted to punch myself. Everything about him changed, and I wished I could have taken the question back, but there was no doing that. He withdrew, mentally, physically. In all ways. Retreating in on himself, he turned his head to stare out over the rolling green hills that made up the boss's estate.

"Not ready."

So much time had passed that I'd almost forgotten the terrible question I'd asked. At those two words, I had to think to understand what he was saying.

Softly, he went on, "She's all I have – *had*. She's all I've ever had, and just to see her like that?"

"I'm sorry."

I came to a stop in front of the house, and he straightened in the seat, looking around. I tried to see the estate through his eyes. The fountain in front. The house itself, a creation of brick and wooden beams, a mixture of classic and modern design. The first time I'd seen it, I wondered if this was what castles looked like.

Since then, I'd seen real castles all across the world.

But this...this was still the most magnificent place I'd ever seen.

This was still home.

But it wouldn't be home much longer unless I managed to talk the man next to me into seeing things the way I *needed* him to see things.

I only had one chance, and it was looking slimmer and slimmer all the time.

In moments like this, I could almost understand Adam's apathy toward the old man. Except he didn't even know the boss.

I did.

And he'd saved me.

13

Reaper

I didn't have to guess where we were. Ninety minutes. If what O was telling was true – and I had a bad feeling it was – then my father lived less than two hours away from me. I couldn't call this a *house* either. It was an *estate*. Nothing else would fit. If the house was any bigger, it just might qualify as a castle.

It was huge. Four stories stabbed into the air with pillars of wood, brick, and glass that was beautiful, classy, and surreal. It was landscaped but not in that touch-me-not kind of way. Everything about the place looked inviting and warm. Like that fairy tale kind of home a kid might read about in a book where some orphans ended up finding out they had a rich, loving uncle or grandfather or something.

But the illusion shattered the second I stepped inside. While there was life outside these walls, once that door closed behind me, it felt like a tomb. I'd been inside plenty of places that felt like death was just a whisper away, and this wasn't any different.

Well, yeah it was.

It was fancier than hell, and when death came calling, he'd have a nice place to hang his hat for however long he was here.

But I don't think death much cares about that.

Everything inside felt cool and quiet, save for the woman at my side.

I could feel her life, pulsing and throbbing. She had more life in her than anything I'd been around in a long, long while.

Inexplicably, I didn't want to go any deeper into the house.

No, what I wanted to do was grab O's arm and pull her out of the house, back to the car. Tell her to drive. We could take her car down and go hit the road, maybe go head down to Eastern Kentucky, head to Natural Bridge or go even farther, down to Tennessee.

Anywhere but here...or to the funeral.

As if she sensed my reluctance, she paused and held out her hand.

I looked down, staring at it.

Then, slowly, I placed my hand in hers, and she curled her fingers around mine.

Strong hands.

Not like mine.

I'd been taught how to destroy, maim and kill with mine, so yeah, they were strong.

But hers were...efficient. Slim fingers, calloused. Neat, short nails. Everything about her was neat, and it appealed to me in ways that I just couldn't explain.

It was like she just didn't mess well with chaos.

It made me want to bring some chaos into her life – maybe by pushing her up against a wall and stripping her naked, pounding into her until she was moaning my name and coming so hard and fast, she forgot her own.

I had a feeling she'd even let me.

I damn well wanted to put my hands on her.

I had a feeling she *wanted* me to.

But now wasn't the time for me to go thinking with my dick.

"This place feels more like a hospital than a home," I said, trying to shift my focus from my cock to...something else. Anything else.

"It didn't use to." She continued to walk, no longer tugging me along by my hand.

But she hadn't let go either.

It was as quiet as a cemetery in the dead of night, silent save for the elegant *click-click* of her heels on the highly polished marble floors. But as we walked, I began to hear music.

Classical music.

We turned one more corner, and O stopped, staring at an open door. The hall led straight toward those doors. Those doors were flung open in an invitation, and there was nothing else in this hall – just those wide open doors.

O didn't take another step though.

She let go of my hand and reached up to rub at her upper lip, her hand shaking a little.

"What's wrong?"

She glanced over at me and shook her head. "Nothing. I'm just...second-guessing myself, you could say. This is either a smart move or a really, really dumb one."

"No in between?"

"Absolutely not." She laughed nervously, then slowly tipped her head back and stared up at the ceiling, her lashes laying thick and full over her high cheekbones. Finally, she swung a look over at me. "You're going to behave yourself in there, Chief Dedman. Otherwise, I'll kick your ass. I don't care if you're a Navy SEAL. You might be a special agent from God's own army, but if you act like an asshole in that room, you're going to deal with me."

"Yes, ma'am." Call me crazy, but I know when a person was protecting someone they love.

She gave me a narrow look, then started forward.

I trailed along in her wake, looking at the art on the walls, searching for some clue as to what I was about to find.

The clues, though, were coming from inside the room itself. They weren't in the hall...I didn't think.

Beep...beep...beep...

My mind cataloged that noise, told me what it was.

My nose had already taken inventory.

Antiseptic smells, although somebody made a valiant attempt to hide it with potpourri and other homey scents. There was also the faint scent of urine.

A woman came rushing toward us. "O, how lovely to see

you. Have you brought..." She looked at me, and her words tripped, then trailed away.

Her face paled, and she stared at me like she was looking at a ghost.

"Nancy, can you give us some time?"

"But–"

"It's okay," O said, resting a hand on the older woman's shoulder. "I'll take care of her. She looks like you just changed and rotated her, yes?"

Nancy nodded.

"I only need a few minutes. We'll read some of the book to her, okay?"

Nancy left, but not without shooting me another dubious look.

But I'd already dismissed her.

Somebody else was checking me out.

The force of her gaze was something to be reckoned with. If she hadn't been confined to that bed, I had no doubt she would have been commanding an army of her own in some shape or form.

Austere intelligence gleamed from those haughty green eyes as we approached, and for a long moment, she didn't even blink.

It wasn't until O stepped in between us that the woman even acknowledged her. There might have been a faint smile, but it was hard to say.

"Hello, Queen Elise," O said, her voice obviously teasing, but there was an undercurrent there.

Not rebuke, exactly.

Warning, maybe. Warning the woman? Me?

"I've brought company, as you can clearly tell. Mind if we sit?"

I watched as the older woman gave two slow blinks.

"Thank you." O gave me a look and nodded at the chair near my right. "Elise – or *Queen* Elise – as I call her, doesn't always hold court. I don't force myself on her if she doesn't want company." She winked at the woman and then nodded at me. "My grandma once told me that if you live to be a certain age, you get to decide if you want to put up with..." O paused, then smiled again, "the bullshit of courtesy that society forces upon a woman. I told the Queen that once. She laughed so hard she almost cried."

That glimmer of a smile came and went as Elise's eyes moved from my face to O's. There was a distinct fondness in her eyes as she looked at the younger woman. I'd never realized just how expressive eyes could be. Then she set that gaze on me, and I realized how *cutting* they could also be. She looked at me as though she saw all my secrets.

They should find a way to duplicate that stare and use it in inquisitions.

I sat there saying nothing while I worked everything into place in my head.

It wasn't until O started shifting in her seat and looking uncomfortable that I realized her friend, *Queen* Elise, was also working things in her head.

"Maybe we should go—"

Elise narrowed her eyes and O obediently sat down. She'd only partially risen from her chair, but at that look, she sat, tucking her hands neatly in her lap, and I couldn't help but think she looked like a schoolgirl who'd just gotten the death glare from some stern instructor.

It tugged a laugh out of me and then I was the focus of that stern glare.

And O's too.

"Something funny?" O batted her lashes.

"I'm just thinking you must have been one hell of a bitch if just a look can make O sit down and shut up," I said, hitching up a shoulder, directing my words toward Elise, not O.

Elise's eyes widened slightly. Then she focused her attention on O, blinked again. This time, each blink was longer, slower.

"She said 'thank you.'"

By blinking? I almost said it out loud, then realized how rude it would sound. The woman clearly couldn't talk, and they'd found ways to communicate without it. Who was I to interfere?

O hesitated, then nodded. After another moment of that hard focus from Elise, she got up and went to the side desk, pulling out a thick stack of white cards. Angling my gaze around allowed me to see that they were almost like the flash cards kids would use when learning to read.

Elise held them up.

A series of cards passed in front of Elise with no response. Then, she blinked hard and fast, three times.

"Is." O nodded and put a card down. The word on it – *Is*.

The same routine continued until she came to another card. *This*.

The last word made my heart hammer, and I wanted to know just what and the hell was going on and how this woman knew.

Him.

Is this him?

O didn't answer the question directly. She just looked at Elise and touched her hand. "I wanted him to meet you. He doesn't understand."

Another session of the blinking and card game had me wanting to cuss a blue streak and hit a wall.

Neither.

Do.

14

Olivia

We were striding down the hall, and Adam moved at a clip so fast, I could barely keep up. Hands in his pockets, he stared straight ahead, and anger practically oozed off of him.

"That's his wife, E—"

"Elise," he bit off. "Yeah, got that. Queen Elise." The bitterness in his voice was enough to choke on. "How long as she been like that?"

"She lost the ability to speak some months ago. She's been confined to a bed for..." I paused and blew out a breath, thinking, "well, longer."

"Why? What happened?"

"Genetics." He pushed through a door, and I followed him out to the gardens, wondering if he planned to keep walking – just walk until his legs gave out. Mine would give out first. I was fit, there was no denying that, but Adam Dedman wasn't *fit*. He was...well, I wasn't sure there were *words* to define him.

There was no spare flesh on him, every muscle defined. He wasn't a walking, talking stack of muscle the way some men are though. He didn't look like he was about to burst out of his skin. He looked lethal and contained and...damn, that ass of his.

He stopped abruptly and spun around.

Reflex had me bringing my gaze up just in time to meet his.

"Genetics? What the hell does that mean?"

Heaving out a ragged breath, I tried to bring my hormones in line. This was so not the time for my libido to decide to wake up from its very long nap. "She has a genetic disorder. It's called Huntington's Disease."

His lids flickered. "Shit."

"You've heard of it."

"TV. Looked it up once." He jerked a shoulder in a shrug and looked past me, and I watched as his mouth twitched into a semblance of a grimace. He started to talk and then stopped, dragging a hand down his face. There were questions he wanted to ask, but something was getting in the way. I don't know if it was his pride – or his faith in his mother.

Taking a step toward him, I murmured, "They'd separated. They...ah...well, they had a son. He died. A drunk driving accident and it was hard on them. Elise was having issues with depression. Her doctor wrote all her symptoms off on that. That's when he met and fell in love with your mother. He was going to file for divorce, but then Elise was in an accident. She slipped and fell. Her assistant was worried she might have tried to commit suicide. Anyway, they were doing tests, and one of the ER doctors saw something. Your dad was called and..."

Adam's shoulders slumped, and he turned away.

"He loves – *loved* – your mother. But as time went by and things started to look bad for Elise..."

"And Elise knew." His voice was thick, caustic. "That's what her question was about, wasn't it? *Is this him?*"

"Yeah. She knows. She didn't. Not right away. But a few years ago, she found out. Elise has a sister." I scowled, thinking of the day I'd walked in on Cherise telling Elise about the *horrible affair* that her husband had been carrying on under her nose for years. It was bullshit. The boss hadn't seen Gena Dedman in years, and he'd never officially met his son, but that wasn't the picture Cherise painted.

You should leave him.

Come be with me. You should be with me. I'll take care of

you.

The boss came clean after that, telling Elise about the affair with Gena, explaining about the child. When I saw her the next day, I could tell she'd spent most of the night crying.

"Anyway, Elise has a sister. She gouges the family for money at every turn, but it's never enough. She wants Elise to live with her because it would be just another way to twist those screws. She's the one who found out about you and..." I finished with a shrug, unable to put it all into words.

"My father." Adam clearly had no trouble finding the words.

"Yeah."

"Shit." He turned away, planting his fists on his hips and staring at nothing. The faded gray cloth of his T-shirt strained against his shoulders, and I could feel the emotions vibrating from him. "So what does he want with me, huh? My mom's gone, but his wife is still alive. Seeing me has to be like a punch to the face."

"She always wanted to meet you, actually," I said softly. "But your mother..."

He turned slowly. "Are you saying the reason I never met my father is because my *mother* kept me away?"

"It was her choice."

I froze, then sucked in a breath at the sound of that voice.

Shit.

Oh. Shit.

Heat flooded my face, followed by a rush of ice and I squeezed my eyes shut as the boss stepped out of a small alcove. The house was huge and even after living here for almost fifteen years, I still didn't know all of its secrets.

How long had he been listening?

As Adam James Clarion met my eyes, I realized he'd been listening long enough, probably from the beginning. The boss arched a brow, his eyes so dark they were nearly black. For a long moment, he didn't look away. Then he turned and met the implacable gaze of his son, Adam James "Reaper" Dedman.

"Hello, Chief Dedman," he said calmly.

"Gee, hi, Dad," Adam said sardonically. There was absolutely no warmth in his voice. No welcome. Then he focused on me. "I'm ready to go."

15

Olivia

"Are you even going to give him a chance?"

We stood outside the car in front of his mother's pretty little cottage, painted white and now gleaming coldly in the light of the dying day.

We'd driven straight to Barrett's office and signed the plea deal with the DA's office.

Adam had a fine of two thousand dollars and eighty hours of community service. Lincoln had snidely informed him that if she'd had *her* way, he would have served out the maximum for his sentence on *top* of whatever Uncle Sam had in mind, but her bosses didn't see the point in prosecuting a highly decorated member of the US Navy.

He hadn't responded, other than to scrawl his name on the line where indicated.

She also told him he'd best make sure that the fine was paid in due time, and he'd stared her down until she looked away. I had to wonder what she had against a military guy because she'd gone and developed a hate-on for Adam before she'd ever really met him.

I'd like to think I was done with Chief Dedman myself, but I wasn't. We'd only just gotten started, and things would be so much easier if he'd just…loosen up.

"I don't see why it matters," he said, finally answering the question I'd forgotten I'd asked. "I don't exactly need a parent in the stands when I'm standing on the pitcher's mound these days."

I clenched my jaw because I knew what he was talking about.

He turned to the walkway, starting up toward the house.

"He was there."

Adam tensed.

I followed him and moved to stand in front of him. "Twelve years ago, you threw the final pitch your senior year. You struck the guy out and won the game. Your father was there. Your mother saw him. They didn't speak. But he was there too. He went to as many games as he could, and he also went to your high school graduation."

"That's a bunch of bull—"

"I was there." Jutting my chin up, I glared at him. "James Clarion pretty much rescued me off the streets, adopted me when I was nine. And from the time I was ten up until you left for the Navy, if you were playing a game and he was home, then he was there. And he took me with him. I didn't know, not at first. It wasn't until I was thirteen or fourteen that I realized he wasn't just going because he loved sports. We lived an hour and a half away, damn it. I could never get his attention like you did. I even thought maybe he was a creeper or something. But I'd known creepers. He wasn't like that."

The anger drained out of me, and I turned away, moving over to the porch and dropping down on the front step to sit. Elbows braced on my knees, I stared at him.

"He just wants a chance. Why can't you give him that?"

"Why is he sending you to ask for him?"

"Because that's what I do. I'm his right hand." Offering a weak smile, I shrugged. "He'll be here to ask you sooner or later himself. But he's..."

I hesitated, knowing I couldn't say anything else. I'd already crossed too many lines by taking him to see Elise.

The tears came on me hard and fast, unexpected. Pressing my fingers to my eyes, I willed them back.

I refused to cry.

Not here.

Not with *him*.

Sucking in an unsteady breath, I waited until my breath was calmer.

When the porch shifted next to me, I didn't dare open my eyes. When the heat of him seemed to scald me through my clothes, I didn't dare look. But then his hand slid up my back.

"Hey…"

I shivered under that gentle, soothing touch.

It was *supposed* to be soothing.

It wasn't.

He did it again, and I had to swallow back a moan.

Get it together, O. It's the physical stimuli, nothing more.

Physical stimuli…that was all. From a man who would have made the Roman gods of old weep with envy – or come after him out of pure spite. Hard, sexy, muscled…intense eyes that could make a woman feel like she was the *only* woman, a mouth that made her *want* to be the only woman, and a body that made her about ready to do anything if he just pulled her up against it.

But it was just physical stimuli.

I spent most of my time invested in the boss and taking care of him and Elise lately. And when I wasn't taking care of them, or whatever else needed to be done with the company, I took care of me, but that usually involved sleeping, reading, or indulging in a little bit of shopping or traveling.

There were very, very few indulgences with guys, especially lately.

And here Adam was. The boy. The man. He was hot and sexy and…

"Look at me, O."

"I'm fine," I said, the words coming out far too unsteady.

Son of a bitch, I didn't *sound* like I was about ready to cry either.

When his hand slid into my hair, I caught my breath.

"O?"

"Please stop, Adam."

The hand slid higher, curving around my neck and the heat of him was like a furnace, melting away tension I hadn't realized I was carrying while filling me with an entirely different sort of tension altogether. "I think you might just be the devil, O. I can't figure out what to make of you."

I eased forward, preparing myself to get up and walk away.

But just as I went to rise, he tugged.

Caught off balance, I toppled backward, and he took advantage. I ended up half spilled across his chest, and he went with the movement, going partly to his back, bracing his weight on one elbow, steadying me with a hand on my hip. "Easy there, O." His gaze studied my face, lingering on my mouth.

I sucked in a breath, and despite the gut instinct that was telling me to get some distance between us – *fast* – I licked my lips instead.

That dark brown gaze tracked the movement, and it was almost like he'd kissed me, because I *felt* the heat of his eyes, almost like he was touching me.

Then he was, that hand on my hip sliding up…the tip of his finger sliding over the lower curve of my lip. I parted my mouth, telling myself I needed to be smart.

But I was always smart.

I braced a hand on his shoulder, my fingers involuntarily curling into the heavy pad of muscle as we gazed at each other.

"This would be a lot easier if you'd just cry it out, whatever it is that's bothering you. I've got a rule about tears and women. I don't take advantage." His voice was a low, rough rumble.

"Maybe you should cry," I said softly. "You're the one who just lost your mom. I don't have any rules."

To my surprise, a faint smile curled that wicked sexy mouth. "You saying you'd take advantage of me?"

Something low and deep twisted in my stomach.

"Might be my only chance. Guys like you don't tend to waste their time on plain Janes." The words slipped out without me thinking about them.

His lashes lowered, shielding his eyes and then he sat up. I had no time to brace myself and ended up on his lap, one brawny forearm pinning me against him. "Plain…" He studied my face, cupping my chin in his hand. "Hey, maybe you'll never walk down a runway, but with that mouth and those eyes…not to mention your legs…"

Heat flushed my face. "No, I'm not going to walk down a

runway, and I'm fine with that. I know what I look like."

"Do you?" He stood up and my weight didn't stop him *at all*. Gasping, I wrapped my arms around his neck, half terrified he'd drop me, but he wasn't even off stride as he turned and moved toward the house. He put me down near the door.

The word *flustered* doesn't apply to me often, but as I stood there adjusting my clothes and smoothing down my hair, I knew that was the *only* word that would fit. Well, *flustered* and *aroused*. I glanced toward my car, the dark maroon Mercedes-Benz the boss had given me when I graduated college. The convertible was my pride and joy, and what I should do was get back inside, drive away, and get control of myself.

If the boss had his way, this would be far from the last I saw of Adam Dedman, and I needed to have my wits about me.

But before I could convince myself to do anything even resembling *responsible*, Adam had the door unlocked, and I was being ushered into the lovely little house.

Still flustered, I said the first thing that came to mind.

"It's like a doll's house. Or a fairy's house."

A laugh escaped Adam as he came up behind me, his hands going to my hips. "Mom would have liked that. She's...she was fussy. Female. She'd put on makeup just to go to the grocery store."

So did I.

"What's wrong with that?"

"Not a damn thing." He dipped his head, and I shivered as he ran his nose along my neck. "I bet you shower and slick yourself down with lotion and primp and put on makeup for the same damn reason."

I wasn't going to tell him that for a long while, I hadn't known what it was *like* to really be clean. So maybe now I went a little overboard. Instead, I replied, "Again...what's wrong with that?"

"Not a damn thing." He breathed in through his nose, and I closed my eyes because he was breathing *me* in and it was painfully erotic. My nipples tightened inside my bra, and I clenched my hands into fists to keep from reaching for him. "Look..."

I opened my eyes, about to ask what I was supposed to

see.

And I saw myself.

At some point in the past minute or so, he turned us, and I didn't even remember him doing it.

There was a round mirror – *mirror, mirror on the wall,* I thought with a half-mad giggle rising in my throat. It hung by the door, a pretty, silver-plated piece that was perfect for checking hair on the way out.

Now I could see myself. My face, slightly flushed, more animated than normal. I rarely let myself *get* animated.

My eyes glittered.

No. I wasn't *pretty*. I would never be *pretty*. But I did have nice eyes. "I'll still never walk down a runway," I said raggedly.

"You don't have to. Striking as you are, people would stare anyway. You look strong...and personally, I think strong is seriously sexy." He turned me around and nudged me up against the door. "The first thing I saw when I walked into that room at the jail was somebody had the wrong person, and whoever she was, was mesmerizing. Then you turned around, and I saw your mouth...your eyes."

He dipped his head, almost close enough to kiss now.

"Do us both a favor and leave, O. My head is in a bad place, and you're not too steady either for some reason," he murmured.

He was right. I wasn't steady. In fact, I was as unsteady as I'd ever found myself. This was Adam. The boy I'd longed for who'd turned into the man I craved. The man who starred in my fantasies. The man I wasn't supposed to touch, yet found my fingers yearning for just that.

Would it really be so bad to surrender to my need? Just once?

Tomorrow, I might not ever see him again. He may refuse James's invitations. This may be my only chance to be with him like this.

I took a deep breath as I decided to simply go after what I wanted, just this once. I pressed my hands to his chest, felt the thunder of it beneath my palm. Proof that he needed me as much as I needed him.

"Then maybe you won't be too pissed off if I take

advantage of you," I breathed, the words almost a whisper.

He blinked once. "Is that what you want to do? Take advantage of me?"

"Does that idea bother you?"

He eased closer, his mouth just a breath away. Then that gloriously crooked grin was back. "Hell, no."

I grinned back and cupped his face with my hand. "Good."

16

Reaper

She tasted like cinnamon, cream, and coffee. I hated cream in my coffee, but I might just start taking it just to remember this moment, how O tasted when I kissed her that first time.

One hand fisted in the short dark hair, I pulled her head back and deepened the kiss.

It wasn't enough, but until she was naked, wrapped around my dick and moaning my name, it had to *be* enough.

Maybe not even then. I might have to have her three or four times before it was enough.

Her hands slid under my shirt, and I broke away to get some distance. She mewled under her breath, but once I peeled the shirt away, she seemed to appreciate it. Then I went to work on her clothes, a white silk blouse that made her golden skin gleam warm and soft in comparison. Her bra was a lacy, silky confection that covered her small but perfect breasts. I was right – she was every bit as strong under those boring clothes as I knew she would be.

Taut muscles flexed in her arms as she reached for me, but I caught her hands, guiding both of her wrists up over her head. "You're too impatient."

Shifting both of her wrists to one hand, I placed the flat of my palm against her torso and stroked down. Her abdomen flexed. Her eyes gleamed, brilliant blue, then her lashes fluttered down as she arched into my touch.

When I reached the button on her plain black skirt, her eyes widened a fraction, then she bit her lower lip, letting it roll out as I tugged the zipper down.

Slipping my hand inside her waistband, I found silk panties...then silken wet woman.

"You wear all these boring, straight-laced clothes, and silk and lace underneath. I'll have a hard time looking at you without wondering just what you're hiding underneath those prim outer layers. And I'll get so hard, everybody will notice."

Her cheeks flushed the prettiest pink.

Then she whimpered, tightening around me as I slid two fingers inside the snug sheath of her pussy.

I withdrew and did it again, harder this time, twisting my knuckles so she would feel everything. I found the rough patch and stroked while my thumb circled her clitoris.

I took her mouth, swallowing her moan, holding down the writhing body that was arching and spasming under my hand. She was there. I felt the muscles clenching, her breathing growing more labored. The intensity in her face and eyes. That's why it surprised me when she caught my wrist just before she went over the edge.

"Not without you," she panted, pushing my hand away.

I tried to ignore her. I like to think that I'm a gentleman – well, at least when it counts – and I don't like to get a woman to this point and stop.

But she pushed against my shoulders, and that's one thing a man doesn't ignore.

Her hair tumbled across her forehead, and she stared at me, her breath coming in hard pants, her bright eyes nearly eclipsed by her dark pupils.

"I don't have anything," I said bluntly.

"Oh." She licked her lips. Then she shrugged. "I do. My...um. I have a bag in my trunk."

Once she said those words – two magical words – *I do* – I twisted my wrist inside her panties and elicited a cry from her.

I didn't *quite* bring her to orgasm, but I had her damn close, leaving her on the edge yet again. When she opened her eyes, I picked her up and carried her to the guest bedroom just off the front door before heading outside to her car.

She was still looking a bit dazed two minutes later when I came striding back inside and tossed the bag down on the bed next to her.

"Get them," I told her, nodding to the bag.

She licked her lips and did as I said while I kicked off my boots and wrestled open my belt and jeans. I could pick a lock, defuse a bomb, and if I had to, I could start an IV. But in the past few minutes, my hands had become so clumsy, I was having a hard time unbuckling my own damn belt or dealing with my zipper.

O reached for me and brushed my hands away.

The foil packet lay next to her. "There better be more than one," I said. If there was only one damn rubber in that bag, I'd have to make a run to the store.

"There's more than one." She tugged my zipper down. She looked so unbelievably erotic, sitting on the edge of the bed, wearing that dowdy black skirt, her sexy silk panties visible through the opening and nothing else. Her shoes had fallen off. Her nipples were tight and swollen, and her eyes were fogged with hunger.

I don't think there was ever a time when I wanted to fuck a woman as much as I wanted to fuck her in that moment.

Nudging her hands aside, I finished the task and grabbed the rubber.

I came down over her as she lay back and scooted farther up onto the bed, but I didn't let her go too far. Grabbing the hem of the skirt, I pulled it down, pausing to kiss her hipbone, the soft skin above her knee, her calf. "You run, don't you?"

"Ah...yeah. Run, swim."

I figured as much. Her shoulders were almost as defined as her legs. She could have been a warrioress, stately and powerful. No...she wasn't *pretty*. That was too boring a word for her.

Sliding my hand up the back of her calf, along her thigh, I cupped one taut ass cheek in my hand and squeezed before levering up onto my knees. She watched as I tore the rubber open, then slowly let her gaze slide down.

I had next to no modesty in me. A lifetime of playing sports, then serving in the military had stripped it away, and being a lover – an *avid* lover – of women had taught me to appreciate the fact that I was strong and fit. But I'd never appreciated it quite so much as when O's mouth parted and her beautiful eyes went a little darker. The pulse in her neck seemed to race faster as I wrapped my hand around my cock and stroked up, then down, pumping a few times before I rolled the rubber on.

She looked up at me, glassy-eyed when I covered her.

Angling my hips, I pressed against her slick folds, and she whimpered, biting her lip as I breached her tight entrance.

"Bite me instead." I flicked my tongue against her lips.

She did – sinking her teeth into my lower lip as I sank into her. She clung to me, her nails penetrating my skin as surely as I penetrated her. And when she was completely impaled on me, it was about the closest I'd ever been to perfection.

But then I moved.

And it got better.

She lifted to meet me as I thrust back in, tightening around me as I withdrew. I shuddered, sweat already forming on my brow.

Hot, breathy little moans escaped her lips, and I swallowed them all down, only dimly aware that I was making some crazy noises myself.

She'd told me she was going to take advantage of me, and I told her I didn't mind.

But suddenly I was thinking maybe I should.

Because I was already in way, way too deep...

Then she wailed as her body shuddered beneath me and nothing else mattered. She clenched down so tight around my cock that I couldn't think or feel or see anything but her.

I didn't *want* to think or feel or see anything but her.

When she cried out my name, I knew I was in trouble.

∽

AT EIGHT-THIRTY-TWO, the doorbell rang.

We were out of rubbers, and if life was fair, that doorbell would be some magical condom-delivering fairy.

But then again, if life was fair, I wouldn't be in Ohio because my mom wouldn't be dead. I'd be back in Coronado. Two of my best friends wouldn't be dead either because we'd saved some high society bitch who hadn't wanted to be saved.

So...life wasn't fair, and the person who'd just rang the doorbell a second time wasn't there to deliver a box of condoms.

Or pizza. I could use a pizza.

I hadn't eaten much since I'd gotten to Ohio, and for the first time, I was actually hungry.

Next to me, O made a low, grumpy noise. "It's not my house. I don't have to answer that, do I?"

"No." Something soft and sweet moved through me, and I shoved it aside because I couldn't do soft and sweet. I didn't even know what in the hell was going on with my life, and I didn't want to feel that vulnerable with anybody, much less O. But I couldn't keep from smiling as I stroked a hand down her hair and got up.

Tugging on a pair of pants, I headed for the door.

I could see a shadow there so whoever it was, they weren't leaving.

Out of habit, I checked everything about the room, although as O had said, it was a doll's house. I'd installed a security system for Mom, and she lived in a nice neighborhood.

Still...who would be here?

I opened the door and found myself staring at a stranger who wasn't a stranger any longer.

Even if I hadn't met him just a few hours ago, I'd know him anyway.

The same dark brown eyes, their shape almost exactly like my own. The familiar nose. The tall frame and broad shoulders.

"Well, I guess showing up twenty-nine years late to the party still counts as showing up," I said caustically.

He inclined his head.

And that's when O stepped into the room...wearing nothing but my t-shirt.

When she saw my father – her boss – she went dead

white.

17

Reaper

I wanted two things. I wanted to know where in the hell O was, and why she hadn't called me back.

And I wanted the sun to come out.

Maybe that counted as three things.

Right now, I'd just be content if the sun would shine while we buried my mother, but that wasn't going to happen either. I could hunt O down after the funeral, but there wasn't a thing I could do about the lack of sunshine.

Mom had loved sunny days, working in her garden or just sitting on her porch and reading a book.

But the damn sun refused to come out.

Surrounded by strangers, I stood there at the side of the dark, ugly pit they'd lower her into, and the press of bodies around me made me feel claustrophobic. I skimmed the crowd, my gaze lingering on the few familiar faces. There weren't many. My gaze bounced off the old guy standing on the outskirts.

He hadn't stayed long last night, hadn't said much.

He and O hadn't spoken more than a few words either.

Now he stared at me with an intensity that even those around us noticed.

Everything inside me relaxed when a hand slipped into mine.

I didn't look over. I'd sensed O's presence just a moment earlier, but hadn't wanted to look away from...

"I don't know what I'm supposed to call him. I can't think of him as my dad," I said as somebody from the church stepped down, and another woman took her place and began to speak about my mother.

"I call him James."

After a moment, I nodded.

"Where did you go?"

But she just shook her head as the woman at the small podium began to talk.

Then it was my turn.

I was wearing my dress blues. Mom had always loved the dress uniform. The collar around my neck felt like it was choking me, and if one more of the nurses made eyes at me, I thought I might lose my fucking mind.

I ignored them and sought out something else to focus on and found myself staring at O. So I talked to her. I told her about my mother, and when I stepped away, people were crying.

The voice of the preacher was an incessant drone in my ear, and I tuned him out, tuned out everything as I thought back over a hundred memories.

We'd gone to an air show and seen the Blue Angels. As soon as we were back in my mom's car, I told my mother I wanted to do that too. She'd hugged me and said, "If that's what you want, then do it." I was eight at the time.

One of our neighbors had served in the Navy during World War II, and she'd let me go over and talk to him. At first, he tried to talk me out of it, but when he realized how committed I was to joining up, he started to tell me stories. I was fourteen when he died, and it was the last time I could remember crying. Until today. I'd broken down and bawled like a baby that morning in the shower.

Mom standing out in the crowd, looking so proud after I'd finished training.

Her voice on the phone when I'd call home after we'd get back to base.

The way she'd looked at Christmas a couple of years ago when I bought tickets for her and her best friend to take a trip to Hawaii.

Then it was over, and I had to keep standing there. I was like a robot, I stood there as everybody came up and offered their sympathy, and I was still standing there long after everybody left. The driver from the funeral home had finally approached, and I was an asshole, telling him to go fuck himself. Idly, I thought maybe I should call and apologize. Mom was just barely dead, and I was saying things that would have made her want to slap me.

Finally, it was just us.

James. My *father*.

O.

And me.

"Why don't you let me drive you home?" she asked.

"What about your car?" Woodenly, I stared at the open hole where my mother now rested. She'd be covered with dirt soon. That wasn't right. I should have cremated her. Maybe taken her ashes to Hawaii. She talked about how much she'd loved it. Or maybe spread them over the garden.

"I came with...somebody. Adam, come on."

She touched my arm.

I turned, ready to go.

But then I saw a tall, familiar shadow, and I realized I'd overlooked someone who had been standing near the back by a tree.

Snapping off a salute, I faced my commander.

Hawkins saluted back and nodded at me. "You're needed back at Coronado."

The grim look in his eyes told me everything I wanted to know.

"Decision's already been made, huh? That was fast."

He didn't try to act like he didn't know what I meant. "Come on, Reaper. Let's get this bullshit over with."

SEALionaire Book 2

1

Olivia

Standing on the balcony, I stared out into the night.

It was late summer, and the sweltering, muggy heat was giving way to the promise of the coming fall. At least it was at one in the morning.

I couldn't sleep.

I'd had a lot of trouble with that lately.

Although maybe *lately* wasn't entirely accurate. It wasn't like it had just started in the past week, or even the past two or three.

No, it had started almost two months ago, ever since a highly decorated Navy officer had emerged to escort Adam Dedman away from the cemetery.

From his mother's funeral.

If I wanted, I could still work up a temper over that.

James, of course, told me there was no point in getting angry. Things had to work themselves out. I wasn't so good at being *calm* these days.

My phone chirped, and I picked it up to check the message, putting it down just as quick. I used to set it to *do not disturb* at night, but for the past few weeks, it hadn't been an option.

Elise wasn't doing so well.

She was running out of time, and soon, James would be forced to bring hospice in. When they came, I'd move back into my bedroom out at the estate. He'd assured me it was my home, and I was welcome whenever I wanted to be there.

I'd almost asked him about *after*.

But things were hard enough on him now, hard enough on all of us. I didn't need to make anything more difficult.

The message was from Tom, a lawyer at a firm that had consulted with the boss recently. We didn't use their firm, of course. I made it a policy not to have personal relationships with anyone I might have to interact with on a professional level. It got too messy. But Tom worked within a different department, and we probably wouldn't work together even if we did hire his firm in the future.

He was attractive, he'd been interested, and I'd been...lonely.

When we bumped into each other at a benefit a week ago, I'd been stupid when he asked me out for drinks. Stupid and lonely, and I'd said yes.

Two hours ago, we were sitting at a beautiful, elegant restaurant perched high on a hill overlooking the Ohio.

One hour ago, he left me at my front door.

Now, he was texting me, asking if I was sure everything was alright.

YOU SEEMED A MILLION MILES AWAY. *I just want to make sure there's nothing I can do to help with whatever is bothering you.*

HE WAS WRONG. I wasn't a million miles away.

I hadn't checked the mileage to Coronado, California – I wasn't that desperate. Yet. But that was where my problem was. Or at least, that's where he was the last time he bothered to call.

When he told me not to bother calling again.

"My life is fucked up enough as it is, O," he'd told me, his voice rough, the words barely audible over the line. "I'm sorry, but whatever James Clarion wants from me, he's just shit out of luck. I can barely handle myself right now, much less anything else."

I texted Tom.

I'M NOT a million miles away exactly, but I do have a lot going on. Too much, and I'm afraid now isn't a good time to get involved in any new personal relationships. I'm sorry.

I DOUBTED I'd hear back.
He surprised me though.

I UNDERSTAND. If you ever want to get together just to talk or have a drink, let me know.

I ALMOST DELETED his number from my phone. He was blond, blue-eyed, and about as far from Adam as he could be.

But I didn't.

Sooner or later, I'd get it through my head that Adam wasn't coming back and then maybe I'd do just that, give him a call.

Maybe.

But I doubted it.

~

"WHAT WILL you do if he doesn't come back by the time..." My heart squeezed, and I let the rest of the words trail off because I simply didn't want to contemplate it.

James looked up from the grapefruit he'd been eating with great reluctance. I didn't see why he hated it. I loved grapefruit. But I'd spent too much of my life eating stale cereal or plain oatmeal, and before that, it had been whatever I could get my hands on. Fresh fruit to me was just as good as candy.

"I've got everything planned out, Olivia. You'll be taken care of regardless, so don't worry."

Annoyed, I snapped a napkin into my lap and took the untouched other half, adding it to the bacon and eggs on my plate. "I'm not *worried*," I said. Frowning, I pointed out, "You realize you've already given me more than enough. You're not obligated to do anything more."

"No, but I want to." The smile he gave me was full of love, and it made my heart hurt. Then he waved a fork around. "Besides, I hate loose ends. You know that. You're meeting the board today, don't forget."

"How could I?" I muttered at my plate, but he heard me nonetheless. "It's like forgetting a meeting with the board of the directors of hell."

"Well, I am the CEO of one of the top defense contractors in the country. It wouldn't do for the board to be made of a bunch of puppies and kittens, would it?" He finished off his grapefruit with a wrinkled nose.

"Does that mean you have to have hellhounds and wild hyenas?" I took a sip of my coffee and watched as he tried not to laugh.

"It's a good thing I selected a mean bitch to take over for me then, isn't it?"

I looked away. "He might still change his mind."

"And they won't accept him right away. You're still the majority stockholder as of now. If things change..." He waved a hand and then glanced at the clock on the wall. "I believe I'll take the rest of my breakfast and sit with the queen for a few minutes."

"Don't let her hear you calling her that," I advised him. I was the only one who got away with it without getting her death glare, a fact that pleased me to no end.

He chuckled. "I wouldn't dream of it."

THE PAST SIX weeks had brought more changes than I liked.

The first had started off when I went with James to a visit to his doctor. He'd told me it was so we could discuss business matters on the way, but I knew the real reason.

He wanted moral support.

He wanted to not be alone as we waited for the doctor to come in and tell us the results.

And I didn't want him to be alone either.

I would have sat there in the waiting room holding his hand if he would have allowed it. But he wouldn't, not with the ubiquitous bodyguards in the waiting room as well.

They went everywhere with him.

He'd told me I'd need to get used to having a pair with me, but I wouldn't, not until I had to.

For the most part, they went everywhere he did, although on rare occasions, like the day of the funeral or the day he'd come to see Adam at his house, he could convince them to wait in the car.

But the doctor's office wasn't one of them, and it wasn't until we were in the room with Hank and Oscar on the outside that I'd taken his hand.

I could still remember how frail he'd felt.

Frail. It wasn't a word I associated with James.

Now, I was the one who needed it. I would have been happier if I hadn't finally acknowledged his point when he said, "They expect to see something specific when they look at the head of the table, Olivia. You don't have to turn yourself into a china doll."

I had shaken my head, giving him a little smile. "I never could."

"No." He laughed. "You couldn't. You're too powerful, too...commanding. So take advantage of that."

On his advice, I found a personal shopper – actually, I found *two*. The first one had annoyed me, and I'd fired her.

The second one...well, I wasn't sure he'd work out either, but he led me into his studio, walked around me, and asked me what I wanted. I'd told him what I didn't want instead.

"The last shopper insisted we find a way to soften my appearance," I told him, saying the words as if they tasted bad. "A makeover, blah blah blah."

He laughed.

"Honey, we don't want to soften a damn thing about you. You're an empress. The whole world should bow down." Then he winked. "History paints Cleopatra as this famed beauty, you know that? But she probably wasn't. She was powerful…and she knew her strengths. I bet you do too. So we'll learn to play up those strengths. And sweetheart, you have them in spades."

All my boring, safe clothes had been relocated to another room so I wouldn't be tempted to drag them back out.

Today, I wore a sleeveless surplus blouse that played up my upper body and made up for the fact that my breasts weren't all that impressive while the high-waisted, full-cut trousers made my legs endless.

No. I didn't look soft or beautiful, but I did cut an impressive figure apparently because several heads turned as I strode across the glass breezeway to enter the boardroom. James was already there. He'd told me to arrive seven minutes late – seven minutes, no more, no less. Several board members liked to arrive a few minutes later as a power play, and he wasn't going to have me waiting on them, not for this.

Make an entrance, O.

That's what I planned to do.

I didn't have any papers with me.

I didn't have any notes.

Everything James and I had planned was already engraved in my brain.

But my throat was dry, and my heart was racing.

The doors opened with a quiet swish, and I stepped inside, my low heels clicking on the strip of marble, announcing my entrance.

A few eyes flicked my way before moving off.

Then they returned, and one by one, every board member turned to look at me.

"Well, it's about time you grace us with your presence, O."

I glanced over at Cherise Whitney – Elise's sister. How I wished she'd sell her shares and move to Italy or France or some other country – she was always jetting about. She sure as hell didn't belong on the board.

Giving her a brilliant smile, I said, "I'm so sorry, Cherise. I stopped in to check on Elise on my way out this morning."

Her face went red.

A few others made commiserating murmurs and asked James about his wife. As the small talk circled around, I moved to the coffee service. Cherise sat there, stewing.

The gloves were coming off today – officially – and she was about to find out.

Cherise was, to put it simply, a cold, calculating bitch and there was only one reason I hadn't already gone head to head with her.

Okay, two.

The first reason was because I knew Elise adored her, and it would hurt Elise if she found out.

The second reason was because James asked me not to – she's the entire reason I met Elise. If I hadn't known her, I wouldn't have known my wife, and my life would have turned out very different.

So he was kind to her even when she didn't deserve it.

But I didn't owe her any loyalties, and James already knew Cherise could only push me so far. The only reason she was on the board at all was because of the shares her former husband had left her. He had been James's partner, and when he died, half of his shares went to her, the other half went back to James. That was part of the reason she hated him so much, I expect. She thought she'd have equal say in this business, but her husband had known her too well.

She didn't have a head for running a business the size of Clarion. She only saw dollar signs. Clarion manufactured arms and worked in the defense industry – there had to be more than *money* to be a success in that world.

Turning back to the table, coffee in hand, I moved to my seat at James's right hand.

He nodded at me and then stood.

"Many of you know Olivia..."

2

Reaper

Bright light scorched my eyes, and when hands came in to grab me, I came out swinging.

"That's enough of that," an irritated but familiar voice said.

It took a few minutes for my befuddled brain to register the voice so I kept swinging.

Overbalanced, it didn't take much for me to end up on my ass and face down on the hard-packed earth. Now I was really pissed off.

Hung over with a pounding head and pissed beyond reason.

Rolling over, I lurched to my feet and brought up my hands, blinking several times to clear my vision.

Hawk and another guy stood in front of me.

A few additional blinks managed to clear my vision enough to tell me who it was. Anthony Vega. A crazy half-Cajun who'd taken Rake's place on the team. The first week he'd been on the team, he'd made up a batch of fried alligator, and I told him I'd prefer to keep my seafood a little more along the lines of catfish and trout.

He laughed at me, told me I could have my pussy fish, but there was nothing like gator meat.

I can't quite figure out how we ended up in a fight, but we'd gone down, and Vega ended up with his new nickname – Gator.

I couldn't look at him without thinking about Rake, and I hated him for that alone.

Memory started to trickle back as I saw his black eye.

I'd done that.

Now I wondered why I didn't feel a whole lot worse.

After all, I was a miserable, ex-special forces piece of shit loser and he was still a US Navy SEAL.

Jerking my gaze away from him, I fought the urge to puke. I didn't want to do that. I had a feeling I'd been doing a whole *lot* of that lately. I could taste it in my mouth and smell it on my clothes too.

Not only was I an ex-special forces loser, I was a drunk. An out of work one at that.

"Come on, Reaper. Let's get you inside and clean you up."

I tried to push Hawk away, but he wasn't having it, and I didn't feel good enough to fight him. We were halfway up the walk when I realized where we were, and *that* was when I started really fighting. "What the fuck, man? What are we doing here?" I demanded.

"You're moving in here. Your mom's lawyer has been trying to track you down for the reading of the will for months. You need a place to live. In case you've forgotten, you've been kicked out of the place you were renting. Nobody back near Coronado will take a chance on you right now, and you don't have a job. So shut the fuck up and get inside."

I flinched at each word, staring up at the pretty house where Mom had lived.

Right up until she died.

My brain supplied the exact number of days that had gone by.

It was a pretty memorable day.

I lost my mom that day.

I kicked my career in the balls.

I was arrested.

I caused a man to die. Hell, I'd been the cause of death for more than a few men, but they were enemies of the country so I could accept those. That dumbass back in the jail had just been too stupid to live, coming at my back like that.

Still, his death didn't sit quite so easy on me.

"I don't want to be here," I said, having to force each word out.

"I'm afraid you don't have a lot of choices, Adam," Hawk said. "You just don't have many places left to go. I found you sleeping in a fucking alley."

"That was just because I haven't found a place yet." Shame burned, crawled in me. Yeah, so I'd been kicked out of my apartment. Not because I hadn't paid my rent or anything, but because I was basically an asshole. Then I'd been more of an asshole and kicked the door in.

The guy who owned the place was one of Hawk's friends, and he'd already told him he wasn't pressing charges. But he also told me I needed to get my shit together.

That was something else that had worked clear of the fog caused by too much alcohol.

Head pounding, I squinted up at the sky. I felt disoriented, like I'd slept a few weeks or a few months of my life away.

"What time is it?"

Hawk snorted. "You'd be better off asking what day it is. We drove pretty much straight across the country, bringing you here."

I shifted my squinty-eyed look toward him and half-stumbled as my equilibrium started to shift around on me.

Hawk didn't offer to steady me.

"Come on. You're going in that house if Gator and I have to drag you. Got it?"

~

THE CLOTHES I found in my old bedroom hung loose on me.

My face looked hollow, and my eyes were so bloodshot, I figured most people would see me and decide I was coming off a week-long bender.

They'd be wrong.

I finally figured out what time – and day – it was.

It was more like a three-week long bender.

"You pathetic piece of shit," I said to my reflection.

I wasn't feeling sorry for myself though. I was pissed off and getting more so with every passing minute. If the fit of my clothes was anything to go by, I'd lost at least fifteen pounds in the past month, all of it muscle. I'd spent most of my time drinking, very little time eating and my brain felt like it was full of holes, like a piece of Swiss cheese, one left out in the sun too long.

I was furious, and as I stood there in the bedroom in the house I'd lived with my mother, shame hit me hard.

I got why Hawk had dragged me back here.

He'd probably known this would happen.

Had to give it to the man. He wasn't my CO anymore – I didn't *have* a commanding officer – but he knew how to read me better than anybody alive.

No CO. No mission.

I was no longer a member of the US Navy. No longer a SEAL.

You have a choice, son. You can face a court martial and I think you know how it will go, or we can discharge you. Right here, right now.

I'd stood in front of two officers, one of whom I'd never even met, and had to listen while they told me my two only choices.

They were right.

I knew how a court martial would go.

I should appreciate that they'd considered certain *facts* – everything that had gone down with the mission that had killed Rake and Dog, then the drunk who'd killed my mom – before deciding to even offer me a choice. And I guess in a way I did.

I didn't deserve that choice, not really. I'd dishonored the Navy, everything I stood for.

And for the past few weeks, instead of sucking it up and figuring out where to go, I laid around like a bum and got drunk off my ass.

A knock at the door had me straightening away from the

sink – slowly. My head still didn't feel like it was attached right. At the moment, my blood probably had more alcohol in it than actual *blood*, and I needed to spend the next week drinking nothing but water so I could get the poison out of my system.

Hawk was standing there, hands on his hips, staring down the hall.

He met my eyes, looked me up and down. "You still look like shit."

"This will make you happy – I still feel like shit."

He smiled. "That doesn't make me happy, son. Come on. You need food."

The very thought made my stomach protest, but he was right. I needed to eat, and there was something in the air that made my mouth water, despite the protest from my stomach.

A few feet away from the kitchen, I stopped dead in my tracks and looked at him. "Shit, did you let Gator into my mom's kitchen?"

"Not like I can cook." Hawk kept walking. "And you're so full of booze, you might spontaneously combust if you got near an open heat source. Quit your bitching, Reaper, and get in here."

Warily, I edged in closer and eyed the table where Mom and I had shared so many meals.

It was empty.

Gator caught sight of me, and his dark face went sly with saturnine humor. "I make the food, dickhead. I don't set the table. Don't worry...I didn't make no gator meat. I'll save that for when you're looking a little less lily-white."

"Suck my dick," I suggested.

He snorted and jerked a thumb at the table. "Get that done or you can eat with your hands."

Gator had a thing for cooking. Before I...left, I'd figured that out. He also believed that people should actually sit *down* at a table when they ate a meal. Somebody had ragged him about it, and he told the guy to take it up with his mama.

Seeing as how my mama and his mama saw things the same, I figured I'd just avoid the headache and set the fucking table. Especially since my stomach had decided food might be a good idea. It was rumbling.

Ten minutes later, we all sat down to eat.

The only thing to drink was water and sweet tea – and the sweet tea was enough to give cavities with one sip. Gator drank half of it himself. I drank the other half.

Hawk stuck with water.

The food was a chicken and pasta dish that settled easily on my raw stomach, and Hawk laid into Gator, telling him how he'd make somebody a great wife someday.

Gator just flipped him off and ate, mostly in silence.

I eyed the black eye, and when he caught me doing it for the third time, I said, "Sorry."

Gator jerked up a shoulder. "Bet your hand hurts just as much as my face. Been told I got a head like a rock."

My hand was bruised, the knuckles swollen. "Feels like I hit a brick wall."

Gator nodded.

He was the one to break the awkward silence again five minutes later.

"You know, you can spend the rest of your life feeling sorry for the fuck-ups you made, or you can do something with your life. Ain't like you don't have the training to do a whole bunch of shit. Plus, you're smart. I mean, you can always go private. Plenty of ex-SEALs do."

"That ain't me," I said, irritated already. I'd joined the Navy to serve my country.

"Yeah, figured." Gator shrugged. "Not surprised. Like I said, you're smart. Plenty more you can do than be a hired gun."

I bent over my food, focused on shoveling more of it into my mouth. But I heard every word.

Problem was, I had absolutely no idea what I wanted to do, and thanks to the spectacle I had behind me, there'd be plenty who gave me a wide berth.

Thoughts like that had put me on that three-week bender.

Feeling even more unsettled, I reached for the glass of sugary-sweet tea and drained it, then got up to get some water to cool the burn in my gut.

"I'll figure something out," I said from the sink.

Sure I would.

3

Reaper

My head was still pounding the next morning. I guzzled another twenty ounces or so of water and hit the pavement, running until my legs felt like putty and I was breathing way too hard.

I had to walk it off and wait for my heart to settle before I could make the trip back home. I'd run for a good forty-five minutes, but that shouldn't have been enough to leave me feeling so wasted.

Unless, of course, I'd spent the past few weeks trying to slowly poison myself with alcohol. There was a good possibility it would take a few more days before I felt even close to myself again.

Whatever it was to feel like *myself* again.

By the time I got home, the sun was creeping up the horizon. No lights were on in the house.

Hawk and Gator were crashing for a while yet – they'd both requested leave. Gator was starting the drive back sometime today. Hawk had said he'd make the determination later.

I assumed that meant he'd be heading back once he was sure I wasn't going to fall back into a bottle.

Pacing back and forth in front of the house, waiting for my breathing to settle, I caught sight of a car coming toward me.

When it slowed, something that might have been both dread and anticipation bloomed in my gut, and I wasn't at all surprised when the door opened, and I saw that sleek, dark cap of hair.

I should have known.

The house had been looking a little too neat, the grass a little too well kept, the flowers all nice and pretty.

As O came toward me, I swiped my hand over the back of my forehead and decided that maybe I'd just go ahead and sit down. Might be easier to hide the raging hard-on I'd developed.

Months.

It had been months since I'd had that long, lean body under mine and I still wanted to feel it again, feel *her*. Taste her.

Turning on my heel, I headed for the porch.

"What did you do, bug the damn house?" I asked. The mean bastard was already showing in my voice, but it was either be mean or...touch her.

"No. Good morning to you, Reaper. Nice to see you, Reaper. Been in town long, Reaper?"

The deliberate politeness in her voice rubbed me raw, and I dropped down on the top step and reached for the bottle of water I'd left there before going on my run. Without saying anything, I opened it and guzzled half. Knowing I'd procrastinated enough, I capped it and looked at my wrist before cursing. I'd stopped wearing my watch back when I'd told myself I didn't need to worry about being called out on missions anymore. Didn't make it any easier to accept it, but the watch had been yet one more punch to the face I didn't want to deal with.

"I don't know what time it is, O, but it's too fucking early to play games. What do you want?"

"Now, Reaper...if I wanted to play games, I'd let you know." She joined me on the step, and the scent of her almost had me drooling, ready to go to my knees and press my face to her neck, her breasts, her lap...her everywhere.

Play games. Please...play games. Or let me play them.

"You going to tell me how long you've been back? Or are you in the mood to play games yourself?" She stared out over the yard, her expression bland.

"Well, let me think." I ran my tongue across my teeth and did a quick mental calculation. "Probably about thirteen hours, give or take."

"Thirteen hours. Give or take." She seemed to turn that over in her head, then nodded. "I don't want to sound rude, but you look like shit."

"You don't." It popped out of me.

It was the truth though. She'd done...something. It was subtle. Her hair was a little different. Softer somehow, but nothing major. And the blocky, ugly suits she'd worn each time I'd seen her were gone.

She wore red.

Power red.

That's what it had to be. The LT was married, and his wife had used that term a time or two. Tina – Hawk's wife – ran her own marketing and promotion company out of her home, as well as raising their son. I was sort of terrified of the woman, if I had to be honest. I can recall a barbeque he'd had at his place once and some of the women had been gushing over a pair of red shoes featured on some website but had hated the price. Tina had said, "Get them and screw the price. Every woman needs a pair of shoes in that shade of red at least once. Power red. It makes the world sit up and notice."

Only it wasn't a red pair of shoes O was wearing.

It was a form-fitting dress that highlighted those long legs and those strong shoulders, and I wanted to peel that skirt up and find out what she was wearing underneath. Then I wanted to get rid of it and bury myself inside her.

Tina was right. That shade of red made the world – and my dick – sit up and take notice.

When I reached over and skimmed a finger over her knee, she slanted me a look.

"You went and added some color to your wardrobe."

"You've seen me maybe ten times in your entire life, Reaper. For all you know, my wardrobe has every shade in the rainbow."

"Nah." Her skin was like silk. I wanted to feel her thighs

rubbing against mine and wondered if I had a chance in hell of getting her naked under me again. Of course, she was here because of...shit. "You're determined to get me to talk to him, aren't you?"

"Bet your ass."

The door opened behind me at that very same moment, and I decided that I was going to find myself some new friends – or new *friend*. I doubted I could consider Gator a friend. Hawk, though...well. Yeah. He was a friend. Had been. Right now, he was on the top of my shit list for even putting me in this position.

Shoving upright, I turned to face him. O did the same, moving with far more grace than I was capable of at the moment.

"Hawk."

I sounded about as irritated as I felt, but Hawk didn't look perturbed or even surprised.

"Hello." O held out a hand.

"Hi. I'm betting you're Olivia."

Narrowing my eyes, I watched as they introduced themselves, or at least exchanged names. Somehow, they already knew each other. When Hawk caught my eyes, he lifted a shoulder. "I had a friend come by to check on the house, but somebody was already doing it. Turns out O had made arrangements. We got in contact."

"So it wasn't just coincidence you were in the neighborhood today," I said sourly.

"Oh, it was." She smoothed a hand down the side of her dress.

Was she doing it on purpose? Drawing attention to her hips, those legs...

Pay attention, dumb ass.

"I didn't know you were coming home anytime soon. If I had, I would have arranged to have the kitchen stocked." O lifted a shoulder and turned critical eyes to the yard. "At least the grass was cut recently, and the roses tended to."

"I can stock the damn kitchen myself," I snapped. "And I didn't *come home*. My *home* is in California."

"Dedman," Hawk said, his voice low.

O didn't so much as blink, merely cocked her head as she

studied me. "Then I assume you'll head back there. You have a job waiting? A house?"

"None of your fucking business."

"That's enough, Chief Dedman," Hawk said, cutting between us.

"I'm not *chief* anything." I shoved at him while the pounding in my head got worse. But the pounding wasn't the only thing going on inside my skull. The voice of recrimination was speaking up too – and not quietly. *You already going back to acting like a jackass? When are you going to grow up?*

"No. You're not. You're Adam Dedman, *civilian*," Hawk said, each word hard and flat, like a slap. "And you were kicked out of your house. You haven't been able to find a job in Coronado, and you won't have much luck finding one there and you know it. Your life there is *over*, man. Why are you trying to pretend otherwise?"

I shoved past him and stalked to the end of the sidewalk, staring down the street.

The sound of O coming up behind me, her heels clicking against the concrete, wasn't really what I wanted to hear.

"Why don't you shower and come for a ride with me?"

"Why?" I was tired. I felt it all the way down to my soul. "I don't want to go and meet Daddy Warbucks, okay?"

"Sooner or later, you'll have to get over this apathy, Adam."

"Back to Adam, are we?" Crossing my arms over my chest, I half-turned, meeting her eyes.

She smiled faintly. "Would you prefer I called you Reaper?"

She could call me pretty much whatever she wanted. Her wide, lush mouth curved up in a faint smile, and I wondered what she'd do if I kissed her.

"Come with me. Whether or not we see Daddy Warbucks will depend on what you think after our first stop." She pursed her lips and shook her head. "Actually, our second. I need coffee. That's the first stop."

"Fine. But only because you said coffee."

"We won't be here when you get back."

Both Gator and Hawk were sitting at the table when I came out of the bedroom, showered and dressed in a pair of khakis and a white button-down that wasn't too wrinkled.

Stopping short, I looked from one face to the other.

The glorious bruise on Gator's face looked even more colorful today.

Both of them looked grim.

"That a fact?"

Gator busied himself with the bowl of cereal in front of him. Hawk looked down into his cup of coffee and then slowly, methodically put it down.

O had declined the invitation to come inside, saying she'd wait in the car and get some work done. It was just the three of us in the house, yet it still felt too crowded as Hawk closed the distance between us.

"Yeah, it's a fact. Listen..." He looked away, his jaw working as he hesitated, apparently not happy with whatever it was he had to say. "You need to focus on whatever it is you're going to do next. Your life isn't over, not unless you decide to keep trying to throw it away, Adam."

The words *fuck you* jumped up, almost flung themselves out of my mouth, but I bit them back.

"I know this wasn't the way you wanted to leave the Navy. But hell, you're alive. You're young. You're smart." He punched me on the shoulder. "It could be a lot worse."

I managed a strained smile.

I got what he was saying in theory.

"Sure, man. Sure."

An awkward silence fell.

I gave him a nod and turned away. Halfway to the door, Gator called out, "Take it easy, Dedman."

I stopped but kept my back to the both of them. "You too, Gator. Sorry 'bout the eye."

And that was it.

My old life was now officially over.

4

Olivia

He was quiet. Too quiet.

After I passed him his coffee, I tried to bring him out of the uneasy silence with an invitation for him and his friends to join me for dinner. "I can cook, or I can take you someplace in the city. I know you're local, but a lot of things have changed in the past few years."

"They're heading out this morning." Reaper spoke in a monotone that revealed absolutely no emotion – and revealed everything.

Tightening my hands on the wheel, I bit back the apology. He wouldn't want to hear it. It wouldn't help.

Then it came out anyway. "I'm sorry everything's gotten so messed up for you."

He snorted. "I'm the one who's messed it all up, O."

"You had a rough time of it. Seemed like you should have caught a break somewhere along the way."

"I had plenty of breaks. I got a slap on the hand for what I did here. I was able to take an honorable discharge. Who knows how many favors my commander had to call in for that? I should have faced a court martial." He stared out the window instead of looking at me, and I wondered if he had any idea where we were. "I walked away from firefight after firefight, watched friends go down. I had plenty of breaks."

Turning the corner, I pulled up to the curb and put the car into park.

Finally, Reaper seemed to notice where we were. The boarded up windows, the lots overrun with grass and the houses that had seen better days, better years...the whole damn place was so miserable, it wouldn't be a bad thing if these blocks were razed and everything was just built all over again.

Maybe the gangs would leave.
Families could come back.
People would have a chance.
"What are we doing here?"
Instead of answering, I opened the door.

A couple of boys barely old enough to shave loitered on the curb. They slid my car an assessing look before even glancing at me. The oldest recognized me and gave me a jerk of his head in greeting. I took the fifty I'd pulled from my purse and tucked it under the windshield wiper, staring at him for another minute before I looked at Reaper. "Come on. I want to show you something. It's just over here."

The church, like so many of the buildings, had busted windows that had long since been boarded over. It hadn't been open for years. "Down there." I pointed to the narrow alley between the church and the house next to it. It was cluttered, filled with garbage cans, a bike, a mattress, and a dumpster.

The dumpster made my stomach ache, even though logically, I knew it probably wasn't the same one.

"What am I looking for?"

"I was found here. I was only a day or two old. They don't know for sure."

For a few seconds, he didn't respond, but then finally, he turned his head and looked at me.

"The preacher who used to serve at this church...it was his wife who found me. She heard me crying, came outside, and there I was." I shrugged, still staring at the dumpster. "They called the cops. They wanted to adopt me but were turned down. I ended up in the system, had some health issues the first few years which meant nobody wanted me. Finally, the system tried contacting the preacher and his wife when I was two or three, but the man had died of a heart attack, and she didn't think she could handle me on her own. So there went my chance...again. Spent the first ten years of my life in foster care. Some weren't so great. Others were pretty decent. Then..."

Taking a deep breath, I turned to Reaper.

"I ended up with one of *those* foster families. The kind you hear about on the news. I wasn't even there a week when he tried to touch me. One of the other girls had told me it might happen, told me I'd be better off to just take it. But...I wasn't very good at that. I screamed. He hit me. I bit him. It got way out of hand, and a neighbor called the police. I ended up at the hospital, and he had this big story about how he came in and saw me attacking one of my foster sisters, but he knew how troubled I was. He'd give me another chance."

The rage on Reaper's face was a cold, quiet one. If he looked anything like that when those idiots in the jail attacked him, it made me wonder how stupid they were.

Looking back down the alley, I rubbed my hands up and down my arms. "They were going to send me back there. I knew it. So I ran. I ended up on the streets. Wasn't all that far from here."

From the corner of my eye, I saw Demarre Karnes approaching, moving in a loose-limbed gait, wearing a black tank top and black ball cap with the brim turned backward. It was almost a uniform. His friend looked practically identical, as far as clothing went. Demarre paused by my car, took the fifty just as somebody came out of a house nearby and called out to him.

The two became three, and when Demarre gave me a sidelong look, I said, "We can't stay much longer."

"And I was having so much fun."

Demarre and his two friends had moved back to their street corner, so I started for my car, Reaper keeping pace next to me. "I was almost eleven when I met his older brother. Jaquan was..." I shrugged. "To me, he was like family. The only family I had. Back then, schools didn't teach you as much as gangs nor do they tell you how much trouble they can be."

We were in the car by now, and I started it up, still staring down the street at Demarre.

When one of his friends glanced our way, I put the car into

drive and pulled away from the curb.

"Even if they did, I was in and out of so many different schools. By the fourth grade, I think I'd attended six different elementary schools. I was smart, but I still struggled to read and keep up. I even *liked* school, but it's hard to keep up when you're always being pulled out and sent somewhere else."

On autopilot, I drove, heading to the next spot without thinking. I'd told him one stop. But he needed to understand.

The playground where it happened had been rehabbed. This whole neighborhood looked different, unlike the sad block where Demarre and his friends still lived.

It was only a span of a few blocks, but it looked like a different world.

There were other cars in the parking lot, mothers with their children, joggers out for their morning run.

I didn't get out of the car though. Just being here made me hurt.

"Jaquan didn't have me doing anything serious at first. He saw a skinny, hungry girl and figured he'd take care of me – and I think he did want to do that. I got to sleep at his place, and nobody could mess with me. If anybody tried..." I shrugged.

Adam looked like he was about to say something, but instead just shook his head. After another minute or so, I went on.

"They didn't last long. He had a lot of girls come, and they stayed because they felt safe with him. That's why. The girls were treated nice. They weren't just toys for the men. But once I got old enough, I had to start helping out. He made it clear that's what I was doing."

Adam raked a hand through his hair. "Don't tell me—"

"No," I said quickly. "I didn't have to whore for anybody, but if I wanted to stay, I had to work. I carried drugs back and forth after I'd been with him a few months. He taught me how to fight, told me that, sooner or later, somebody would try to hurt me, and I'd have to hurt back. I was always thinking that it would be like it had been with that guy."

"Your foster father."

I looked at Adam. "Yeah."

I lapsed into silence, staring out the window.

The bench was still there.

"Jaquan brought me here one Friday. Told me it was time I got serious. I told him I was; told him I'd do whatever he needed me to do. He hugged me, said he knew that, which was why he'd picked me to do this one."

I closed my eyes and could see that moment clearly in my head.

"So Jaquan wanted me to go up to this 'old dude,' as he called him, thinking he'd help a little kid like me. He said that all I had to do was distract the man, and he and Bianca would take care of the rest."

"Take care of the rest?" Adam asked. "That doesn't sound good."

I shook my head. "I had no idea what he was going to do. I'd never seen them really hurt anybody before – at least nobody who hadn't tried to hurt them first. So I was out there at the park, walking around like they said. And this old guy was out there, just like they said he'd be."

I blew out a breath as the memory played out in front of me. I remembered how hard my heart was beating, how cold my fingers were.

"I went and asked him for some money, told him my mom had kicked me out and that I was hungry. He looked like he wanted to cry and said he'd get me money. He also said that, if I wanted, he could even find me someplace to live, a family."

Even now, I could remember the look in James's eyes as he said it. The intensity – the sincerity.

And then I remembered the look of pain after Jaquan shoved a knife into his side. Bianca pushed him down and grabbed his wallet while Jaquan grabbed my hand and told me to run.

So I ran. But then at the corner, I saw a police car.

And instead of running away, I ran to it.

"Your father spent six hours in surgery because of me. Six hours in surgery because he had a habit of going to one of the roughest parts of the city and handing out money, trying to help kids who didn't want help."

Reaper was staring out the window.

"I ended back up in foster care. I could have run away, but I was afraid. If I ended up back on the streets…"

"You were afraid of what might happen there because of this Jaquan guy."

"Yeah." I stared at the bench for another moment. Then I put the car into drive.

"So how did you come to work for him?"

"Two weeks after I saw him on that bench, he found me in the system and asked if I'd like to have a home – a real one. I told him he was crazy. He said it was possible and would I please answer the question." I glanced over at Reaper before pulling out of the parking lot. "He filed to become my guardian. I've been with him ever since."

5

Reaper

O was making it harder and harder for me to just dislike the son of a bitch.

I could handle that though. There were plenty of people I didn't dislike but still had no desire to have any connection with. They could exist in the world, and I could exist in the world. I didn't have to know them.

But she was making it harder for me to ignore *this* connection.

The connection to the man who fathered me.

It was one thing when he'd just been some unknown faceless bastard who'd knocked my mom up and then walked away from her – from *us*.

Then I find out that he'd been married to another woman when he met and fell in love with my mom. On top of that, I learned that he was even considering divorce before tragedy kicked everybody in the teeth and his wife was diagnosed with a chronic illness.

Now...

Yeah, I wanted to know him.

I wanted to look this man in the eye and try to understand him.

Understand how he was able to take a girl off the streets after she helped, even unknowingly, a couple of street toughs almost kill him, then raise that girl as his own, turning her into this elegant, classy lady?

How could he do all that, be all that, and yet not have anything to do with me? I was his *son*, if O was to be believed, and yet we had no connection.

Nothing.

I needed to understand.

Brooding at the window of one of the tallest buildings in Cincinnati, I stared down over the city and tried to convince myself otherwise.

I wasn't having any success.

Other things were going on in my head too.

Like who the man was.

She'd given me his name, and if I'd heard it at any other time in my life, I might have already put two and two together, but now wasn't any other time in my life.

Now was now, and I was just now getting it.

I was just now putting two and two together after walking through a metal detector, turning over my ID, and getting a guest pass to walk into one of the most secure buildings in the Cincinnati area.

Clarion Arms and Securities.

James Clarion.

Apparently, my father was the primary stockholder of one of the biggest arms and defense contractors in the country. He had contracts with US, Canada, Mexico, not to mention military units in Europe and Asia.

James Clarion.

My father.

"Why now?" I asked quietly when I heard the phone hang up.

O didn't pretend not to understand.

"Because it's time," she said simply.

"Yeah? What made him think *now* was the time? The fact that my mother is dead and can't stop him? Or is his wife getting worse?" I turned and met O's serene, steady gaze and tried not to think about how I'd seen those beautiful blues looking anything but serene and steady.

"It has nothing to do with Elise. She would have been fine if you had met James years ago."

"Yeah, right." I snorted and turned back to the window. "I'm sure she would have loved to meet me, the product of her husband's indiscretion. I doubt she even knew I existed until you dragged me to her bedside."

"She's known about you almost since your birth." O's voice was cold, almost clipped.

Turning to her, I met her eyes and realized she was serious – deadly serious. Tucking my hands into my pockets, I rocked back on my heels. O's arms were crossed over her chest, and she was tapping her nails against her arm.

"You're not a dirty secret, not to either of them. Elise was the one who actually *told* me about you," O said loftily. "And to be quite honest, she was very envious of your mother. The queen..." O paused and licked her lips, looking away for a brief moment. When she finally looked back at me, she was sad. "She wasn't able to have any more children other than the son who died. I think she would have...welcomed you."

I clenched my jaw against the urge to point out that I *had* a mom, a damn good one.

It seemed spiteful and ugly, especially in the face of O's quiet pain.

"You love her," I said.

She just looked at me, but the answer was there, written clearly in her eyes.

Aggravated by everything she was forcing me to face, I skimmed my hands back over my hair and turned back to the window.

"Fine." I bit the word off like I was chewing nails, and it tasted about the same to me – bitter and sharp. But I didn't see much choice. I could keep refusing the inevitable and be an asshole, or just give in. It was sounding more and more like the reason I had for not wanting my father in my life wasn't true, so what other excuses was I going to make for myself?

"Adam?"

I didn't look back at her. "You heard me," I said sourly. The pounding in my head had faded away to a dull ache, but now it was back in full swing, and I was tempted to slam my head against the window and give myself a *real* headache. If I hit hard enough, maybe I could knock myself unconscious and wake up after all the poison had left my system.

Then I could think better and figure out a way around this.

There wasn't one though.

And I knew it.

"Well, then. How about lunch?"

I shot her a look. "Lunch...is that code for you and me finding a room?"

She arched a brow. "No. That's code for you and me meeting up with James. I think we've waited long enough, don't you?"

"I like my idea better." Letting my eyes drift down over her body, I made no attempt to hide what I was thinking. "I keep trying to figure out what you're wearing under that dress."

"Nice attempt at distracting me." She picked up her phone as she sat.

"I take it that you're not going to change your mind."

She didn't answer – not me, anyway. "Hello, boss. Do you have plans for lunch?"

I turned back to the window and crossed my arms over my chest, settling back into my brood. It wasn't as easy as I'd like. The one-sided conversation kept distracting me. Once she'd set a time and picked a restaurant, I debated on whether I should just leave. I could kill time walking around the city and not torment myself.

She hung up just as I managed to convince myself to do just that – walk out and let the very efficient and slightly scary secretary I'd met earlier know I'd meet them at the restaurant.

But when I turned, O was on her feet, moving to the door.

"See to it that we're not disturbed, Grace. Mr. Dedman and I have some matters yet to discuss," O said, one hand resting on the door.

"Of course, Ms. Darling."

When O turned back to me, she looked a little uncomfortable.

I had a good idea why too.

"*Darling?*"

"Yes?"

I forced myself not to smile. "Is your last name really

Darling?"

"*Your* last name is *Dedman*." She put her hands on her hips. "You got a problem with my last name?"

"Absolutely not." I took a look around the room, taking note of the fact that I didn't see a single name placard. I'd been in enough offices to know that most bigwigs usually had their names hammered out on something. Although...I took a closer, more thorough look. The office actually looked fairly new. Smelled of paint. There were things in a box along one wall. "Is this a new office?"

"What's that got to do with anything?"

"Just wondering why you don't have some shiny piece of brass on the desk with your name on it, Ms. Darling." I hooked my fingers in the neckline of her dress and drew her closer.

"Good eye." She licked her lips. "New office, Chief Dedman."

"Don't–"

She laid a finger on my lips. "How about you stop talking and kiss me?"

I looked down into those gorgeous blue-purple eyes and felt something deep and raw twist inside of me. She licked her lips again, and I was lost. "Yes, ma'am."

Her mouth was every bit as sweet and soft as I remembered, her body as strong and sexy. She came to me, wrapping her arms around my neck, her tongue curling against mine in a way that made my brain go into a slow meltdown.

Catching the hem of her snug fitting skirt, I smoothed it upward and found the answer to my question.

Panties...silk and lace.

That's what Olivia Darling wore under that sexy as sin dress.

Easing back, I nudged her up against the desk, so I could tug her panties down. She bit her lower lip, glancing at the door.

I followed her gaze. "Want me to stop?"

"No. Why else do you think I locked it?"

"You really do want to drive me crazy." I continued on my mission of getting her naked, and once I had that slip of material off, I tucked them into my pocket. She remained where she was, half lounging against the desk, her dress pushed up over her hips, wearing a pair of sexy heels while her hair spilled into her face and eyes.

Leaning in, I nuzzled the neat thatch of curls between her thighs, then licked her.

O moaned, her head falling back.

I did it again, grabbing one thigh and pushing her legs open so I could taste her more completely.

She whimpered and rocked closer, hampered by her angle, the desk.

I boosted her up to sit on the edge, and she gasped.

Shooting her a look, I asked, "We okay?"

"The desk...granite. It's cold." Her eyes were hooded, smoky with hunger, hidden with...other things.

"You won't be cold for long," I said softly.

Then I began to feast on her like she was a banquet and I'd been denied way too long.

She muffled her moans behind her hands, and when I knew she was about ready to come, I lifted up and braced myself over her. "You got a condom?"

O shook her head, her hands coming down to rest on my chest a moment before starting to slide in a southerly direction. "But we don't need it...unless you've been misbehaving since your discharge. I..." She touched her tongue to her upper lip then shrugged. "I started taking the pill about a month ago."

"That a fact?"

She nodded. "Everything else is fine too. Are you?"

I spread my hand out over her throat, used my thumb to tilt her chin up. "There's a hell of a lot of reasons we should use a rubber, aside from the obvious. But I don't give a damn. Take me out. I want to feel your hands on my cock."

O's gaze went hotter, sultrier, and if heat alone could do a man in, I would have come all over her in that moment.

She took her time, dragging my zipper down before sliding her hand inside my pants, closing her fingers around me, stroking down. Teasing, taunting little moves that had me driving into her hand, and she responded by twisting her wrist when the head nearly left her grip. It was erotic and intoxicating, and if we'd been someplace else, anyplace else, I might have stripped her naked, straddled her and had her stroke me until I came, then stroke me hard again so I could make her come.

But we weren't in a good place for all of that, so I shifted around and caught her wrist, dragging it up over her head. "You keep that up, and you won't be able to leave this office without looking like you've been anything but good and fucked."

Her mouth parted and her eyes went dark. "Maybe I don't have a problem with that."

"Don't tempt me, O." I bit her lower lip and thrust into her, hard and fast.

She cried out, the sound smothered against my mouth.

I swallowed it down as I drove into her, shifting high on her body so each drag of my hips had me riding against her clit. A subtle flush appeared along the neckline of her dress and rose higher, along her throat then her cheeks.

She jerked against my hold, even as her body pushed against mine.

A battle – the best damn kind.

Catching her other hand, I stared into her eyes as I pinned her down, looking for some sign I should let go. There was no letting go. Instead, O just reared up from the desk and sank her teeth into the pad of muscle along my shoulder.

Control threatened to shatter, then break.

Her pussy gripped me, milked me with each thrust and I thought I just might die, she felt so good.

When she finally started to come, I buried my face in her hair and released her wrists, wrapping my arms around her torso, half lifting her from the desk in an effort to get even closer.

She moaned my name.

Just as my cock pulsed inside her snug cunt, I heard it.

My name on her lips, a low, sweet moan.

"Adam..."

6

Reaper

The restaurant was a pretty little place across the river.

We'd taken the walking bridge and had already been seated for several minutes when the man finally approached.

I sat with my back to the wall so I could see him coming. I pretended otherwise, feigning an interest in a menu, although the minute I looked up from it, I had absolutely no idea just what I'd been reading. It could have been offering dead cat brains and rotgut for all I knew.

James Clarion kissed O on the cheek after she'd risen to greet him then insisted that she seat herself before he took his own chair.

That was the chair directly across from mine.

It was a small, three-seater table, and I wondered briefly if O had requested one of the chairs be removed so we'd all be seated at an equal distance from each other.

Now, sitting there staring at James Clarion, I tried to figure out what to think, what to feel.

I knew a little more about him now. His name had rung a bell – or twenty – and it would have taken more willpower than I had to resist digging around to see what I could find.

And I had to wonder...just how distant had he really been from my life?

There had always been *enough* in my life. When Mom's car broke down, she had the money to fix it. If I was playing ball, I had the money for the equipment I needed. Then I started receiving offers from schools I'd known we'd never be able to afford – except Mom had told me if I wanted to go, she'd make it happen.

I'd chosen the military instead, but she'd assured me whatever choice I made, college or any other road, money wouldn't be a concern. And I'd had a nice truck for a graduation present. It wasn't a flashy supercar or anything, just a reliable truck that had gotten me from point a to point b – and when I was done training and shipped off to my first base, it had gone with me.

"You gave my mother money to help raise me, didn't you?"

James Clarion was one of the richest men in America, and he had one hell of a poker face. As he returned my level stare, I couldn't tell if I'd surprised him or not. After a brief pause, he inclined his head. "Yes. You are my son, after all."

I'd gone my entire life without a father, and I hadn't even really resented that fact. My mom had been enough – had always done her best to *be* enough. Now, sitting across from the man who'd apparently loved her, I tried to figure out what to say next.

I stared at him, hard. I found it more than a little disconcerting to know that I looked like him. Or at least I would in another thirty years. We shared the same dark eyes. His hair was mostly steel gray, but it was mixed in dark brown or black. My hair. His was longer than mine. After so many years in the Navy, it felt weird to let mine grow out, so while mine was just a little longer than what military regulations deemed acceptable, his brushed his collar.

My mother had been average height, five foot five, fair, and what she liked to call *plump*. She was a cute and curvy thing when she'd been younger. I'd seen pictures, and I could even remember guys flirting with her, although I'd been too young to know what flirting was.

I was tall, right at six-three, and judging by the way James

Clarion looked now, I knew where I'd gotten my build from.

He had an austerity to him that should have seemed foreign, but it wasn't. I held myself like that. Maybe not with quite the same...class. He had this weird sort of reserved dignity to him, and now I found myself wondering how Mom had even met this guy.

"Why weren't you ever in my life?"

James lowered his gaze then closed his eyes. He seemed to slump, become older, more frail. It lasted for all of ten seconds before he looked back at me. "It was your mother's wish. I had to honor it."

"Had." I snorted and looked away. "You didn't *have* to do shit."

"I did. You see...I loved your mother." His voice softened. "She was the love of my life. There were so many things I couldn't give her, but...I could give her that. I could respect her wishes."

"Why would she not want me to know my own father?"

"I can't claim to understand why she wanted it that way, Adam." He rested his hands on the table and started to say more, only to pause when the server approached.

I lapsed into brooding silence, tersely giving the server my order and waiting for the others to finish. They were in a chatty mood, and it took a few minutes for the young woman to move along. I was ready to chew nails by the time we were alone again.

Silence stretched out, and I was about ready to shatter it – with a fist if necessary – when a voice broke it. But it wasn't James.

"It's possible she was too embarrassed, Reaper," O said. "Either that or she feared it would be too confusing for you when you were younger. Then as you got older...?"

I looked at her skeptically.

She lifted a hand. "I didn't know your mother. But if I'd had an affair with a married man, even if he was planning to divorce his wife, I'd be embarrassed. I'd hide it. If there was a baby...? I can't even imagine. Maybe she planned on explaining when you got older, but it just became harder and harder. It was one big lie, and it kept snowballing."

Now something entirely different tightened inside me –

confusion. Doubt. My mother wouldn't have done that, would she?

7

Reaper

"We met at a bar."

After O's possible explanation, we'd had an unspoken agreement to move into safer territory for a while. But once we'd finished eating, I'd finally asked the question that had been burning in my mind. How they had met each other.

He didn't look surprised at my derisive look either.

In fact, he smiled.

"Laugh if you want, but it's how we met. That was a difficult time for my wife and me." Now he looked away, and for a few moments, he said nothing. When he did look back at me, some of the cool façade looked a little fractured. "I have no desire to make excuses or rationalize what happened between your mother and me. I can't even say I regret it or that it was a lapse in judgment. It resulted in you, and neither your mother nor I regretted that for a moment."

I clenched my jaw and looked away.

"What I do regret is that my actions caused my wife pain."

"Should have thought of that before you tomcatted around on somebody with a terminal illness," I snapped.

"We didn't know."

Whipping my head around, I looked at him, then at O.

O was sipping from her glass of wine, and I tried to think.

What had she told me that day? Had she told me that part?

James continued. "Elise had been having certain symptoms, mind you. Mood swings. Some forgetfulness. But most of it could be written to..." He paused, a thoughtful frown creasing his face.

"To her being Elise," O said with caustic humor, lifting her wine glass in toast. "Long live the queen."

"To the queen," James echoed, lifting his water glass. He cracked a smile. "And yes, it could be attributed to her being Elise."

James looked over at me. "Elise would be the first to tell you that she isn't always the easiest person to be around. She can be temperamental, to say the least. Before she was first diagnosed, the mood swings and depression were...awful. They were the source of many of our fights. Then our son died and..."

He shook his head and cleared his throat, coughing into his napkin. He took a long drink of his water before going on. "Things grew worse. I encouraged her to get help, to see a doctor. Finally, we separated. During that separation, she did go to the doctor – several of them. You see, early on, she was still herself. It wasn't until some of the early physical symptoms kicked in that anybody realized there was a problem."

He gave me a tired smile.

"There was little family history to go by. Elise's father was killed in WWII, and her mother died when she was very young. Both Elise and her sister were raised by a distant cousin. Whether or not there was a family history, nobody knows."

"I'm sorry." The words were out of my mouth before I knew I was going to say them. James nodded and seemed to age another few years as he sat in front of me. Finally, he went on.

"We were considering divorce when I met your mother. Both of us were seeing other people, although none of the relationships Elise had were serious. Had life not been so cruel, Elise and I would have likely divorced and I would have asked your mother to marry me."

I cleared my throat, still unsure what to think or feel. "I get the sob story. It was a lousy deal all around."

"I would have given a great deal to be able to know you growing up," he murmured.

"Oh, please." I didn't even feel bitter as I said it. I was almost thirty and had long since come to grips with life as I knew it – at least up until I fucked myself over. The fact that I hadn't known my father hadn't scarred me irreparably. Seeing how some of the kids I'd known had dads who weren't worth two shits put together? Sometimes I felt like I was the lucky one because my mom had been amazing. I'd made peace with how things were.

Leaning forward, I braced my elbows on the table and met James Clarion's eyes with my own, trying not to think about how alike they were. "Here's the thing. At some point, I probably would have given a great deal to have known you. But that time has come and gone. I don't need a dad to be there at my graduation, to help me fix a car, or stand out there when I'm getting back home from leave. I don't need you."

I stood.

"Perhaps I'm the one who needs you."

I went still. For a few seconds, I let that turn over in my head, then I said, "Maybe you should have thought about that before you ignored me the past three decades. Relax, Mr. Clarion. You've got Ms. Darling here, and she seems very loyal. I imagine she'll be happy enough to stay by your side for the next twenty or thirty years, or however you–"

"The doctors have given me three months."

I didn't quite make it to the door before those words penetrated.

I almost stumbled.

Nearly tripping over my oversized feet, I turned and stared at Clarion from across the room.

He was studying me with calm eyes.

O was staring down at her lap, twisting her napkin around her fingers again and again. As I watched, she took a deep, bracing breath and her shoulders hitched twice before she calmed herself.

Finally, she lifted her head and met my eyes, and I saw the truth of his words echoed in hers.

"What do you have?" I asked, surprised at how easy it was to ask. "Cancer?"

"Yes. Pancreatic. It's...virulent. And I prefer not to spend my final months fighting the inevitable. I want to enjoy what little time I have left. I want to spend it with my wife, with O." He inclined his head, and I heard the unspoken words in his voice. *With my son.*

"Why the hell are you telling me this now?" I demanded roughly. "You had years to come to me and tell me who you are. You could have done it. Just you. Mom didn't have to know."

"I..." He took a deep breath then and finally looked away. "I don't know. I have no answer for that, save for the fact that I was afraid."

8

Olivia

He was in the backyard again, trimming his mother's roses.

Dirt streaked his forearms, sweat streaked his face, and rage permeated his very being.

I waited there, leaning against the fence. He knew I was there, but he was either ignoring me or just too pissed off to talk.

Finally, he hurled down the long, wicked blade he was using to trim back the pale pink blossoms and turned to face me, hands on his hips. "What?" he demanded, chin up, tone belligerent.

"He's a good man, Adam," I said softly.

"I don't care if he's a good man. I just want to be left alone." His jaw was tight, his dark eyes shut down. But the misery in him beat at me.

Shoving away from the fence post, I moved toward him. His lids flickered, eyes dropping down to run across my body. I felt the warmth of that look as though he'd reached out and touched me. I wished he had, hoped he would.

"I think he's left you alone long enough." Lifting both of my hands, I placed them on his chest, felt the ragged beat of his heart against my palms. "But he's not why I came here."

Reaper reached up and caught my wrists, holding them still. "Careful. I'm not feeling very nice right now."

The heat in his words set my heart to racing. "Promise?"

A low snarl escaped him, and he jerked me close.

He didn't kiss me though. His mouth was a breath from mine, and I could smell the earth and sweat on him, and faintly...roses. It shouldn't smell so intoxicating on a man, but it did. It filled my head in a rush and made me want to bite him.

Would I ever smell roses again without filling this insane rush of lust?

"You should go now," he told me. "Before you do something that really pushes me over."

I eased in closer, flicked my tongue over his lower lip. "And just what would really push you over?"

His fingers tightened on my wrists.

"O..."

"Adam." I kissed him this time, a light teasing brush of my mouth over his. I wanted to touch him, but he still held my wrists in a tight grip, and I couldn't get away. "What happens if I pushed you over?"

He let go of both wrists and in a split second, he had them jammed into my hair, and my head was cranked back.

"This."

I didn't even have time to brace myself before his lips crashed into mine. The world faded away into a blur, things turning into white noise and red-hot heat. Vaguely, I recall him lifting me and telling me to hold on.

Then I was trapped between him and something else – hot, hard, smooth. The garage.

My skirt was yanked up, my panties yanked away.

"Adam," I said, my voice shaking.

He stroked two fingers down my slit. "You're already wet. Is this for me?"

"Yes." Groaning, I let my head fall back, shuddering when those two fingers penetrated me, pumping in and out. "Oh. Please don't...please don't stop."

He twisted them, screwing his wrist as he thrust deep inside me and I felt each nuance, each of his fingers pushing me closer and closer to the edge.

I clamped down, already so close to coming. Needing the release badly. Everything inside me tightened as he stroked my g-spot, the heel of his hand pressed against my clit.

"Stop."

Dazed, I stared up at him, trying to understand.

He'd stopped. He told me to stop.

I didn't... "What?"

"I want you to come around my dick like that. Nothing else – unless it's my face, later on."

I went red at the image, even as parts of me threatened to melt all over again.

The rasping of his zipper seemed terribly loud, and I looked around. "But...Reaper, we're outside."

"I know. We're fine. It's private."

I looked around, still nervous and realized that three sides were completely shielded, one by the garage, two by the trellis. The third faced out over nothing, absolutely nothing.

My skirt was twisted in his hand, and he dragged it up. My knees went weak, and I sagged back against the wall. But Adam caught my hip and tugged me in closer. I started to wrap my arms around him, but he turned me around and guided both hands to the wall, nudging me forward.

His cock passed over my ass, then the head slid down my slit, probing me while spreading the slick moisture of my arousal.

"I'm not wearing a rubber, O. You've gone and pushed me too far to care. Last chance..."

"That boat has come and gone," I whispered, then cried out when he drove in, not caring that we were outside, where anybody could hear.

Reaper slid a hand around my hip, arrowing straight down, and when he brushed my clit, I twisted against his fingers, blinded by the pleasure. "Please, oh, please..."

He grabbed my hair and turned my head until our mouths met, his teeth biting and nipping at my lower lip. I was panting, struggling to breathe, pleasure crashing into me until I came.

Letting go of my hair, he grabbed my hips and thrust harder, not giving me time to recover. His fingers dug into my skin as our bodies slapped together, the music of our lovemaking filling my ears.

He pressed the tip of his thumb against my anus, and I clutched at the side of the garage, needing something to hold onto.

"You feel so good," he whispered and breached the tight muscle, filling me everywhere, overwhelming me with all the different sensations moving through me.

"Please..."

His hand was in my hair again, pulling my head back, taking my mouth while his cock and thumb thrust into me in tandem. I was pressed into the building, taking what he was giving me, and loving it.

"Please what?" he said against my lips.

I was whimpering, so full, another orgasm quickly approaching, rushing at me like a speeding train. He moved harder, faster, his thick cock skewering me over and over.

When I came, I bit into the fist I'd pressed into my mouth to muffle the scream.

9

Olivia

"What are you going to do?"

Reaper lay against my back, and when I spoke, he groaned and buried his face in my hair. After a few seconds, he said, "I'm going to lay here for a few more minutes, then I'm going to drag you under the shower outside and fuck you again."

Rolling to face him, I reached up and cupped his cheek. "That's not what I meant."

He kissed my palm. "I know what you meant, O."

I didn't think he was going to say anything else. But after a few minutes, he swung his legs over the double wide chaise lounge we'd flopped on. It was tucked under the broad shelter of the roof of the little shed where his mother had kept her tools for her garden. It wasn't some boring old work shed, either. He'd turned it into a beautiful little space with lights, chairs, a mini fridge, a porch with a roof, and the chaise lounge. I'd seen these before – she-sheds, they called them online. He should have looked ridiculously out of place in all the fussy, frilly femininity, but he just looked more insanely masculine. Sitting there with his muscled back rigid, Reaper stared out over the yard. The blue-green water of the pool rippled, beckoning like an oasis.

"I don't want this mess, O," he said softly. "My life is

enough of a mess as it is. I don't even know what to do with myself now, and he's got me dealing with...this."

I didn't want to complicate things even more, so I stayed quiet. But James wasn't just looking to connect with his son. He wanted that more than anything, but there were...other things.

Stroking a hand down his back, I debated on what to tell him and finally decided I couldn't *not* say anything. "You realize that in a few months, he'll be gone. Your life will still be complicated, and you've got plenty of time to think through what you're going to do. But you won't have him. This is pretty much the only chance you have. And he's a *good* man. Do you want to give up this one and only chance?"

"*He* had a hundred chances – no, more. What's three-hundred-sixty-five times twenty-nine?" he asked, sarcasm thick in his voice.

"He explained why he waited."

"Shit." Shoving upright, Reaper started to pace, moving to the door and staring out for a moment before coming back to look down at me. The indecision in his eyes left me feeling bruised. I couldn't imagine what it was doing to him. I didn't want to.

Rising, I wrapped my arms around his neck and kissed him.

He stayed rigid, unyielding.

When I pulled back, the blue of the water caught my eye yet again.

So I took his hand. "Come on."

He didn't move at first, but I kept insisting.

"You know what?" I said as we drew closer to the pool. "I've never once gone skinny-dipping, Adam Dedman. Not once."

He glanced around. "It's not even five o'clock, O. The privacy fence makes it harder for people to see, not impossible."

I grinned at him as I pulled off my dress. "If they're looking, then it's their own damn fault. Come play, Reaper."

I turned and dove in, started to swim.

When he joined me a minute later, something inside eased.

Then he caught up with me and wrapped me in his arms, taking me down, our legs tangling, his mouth fusing over mine. Just when I thought my lungs would burst, he gave a few powerful kicks, and we broke the surface of the water.

"You want to drown me," I muttered against his lips.

"Relax...I'm CPR certified and then some. Take a breath."

I did. We were back under the water in seconds, and he stole my breath again.

~

"I'LL GIVE IT A CHANCE," Reaper said over a dinner of pizza and cheap beer.

I loved the pizza, hated the beer and almost choked on a sip when he said those words, so casually he might have been discussing the weather.

I grabbed the can, took another drink, a healthier one, the taste enough to make me gag, but at least I stopped feeling like I was going to choke on my shock.

Putting the can down, I swiped my hands on my jeans, then left them there so I wouldn't fidget. "Yeah?"

Reaper drank some water from a bottle – he'd told me he was cutting back on the alcohol. I should have asked for water myself, but when he'd asked me if I wanted a beer, I'd replied on autopilot, not expecting something cheap enough to peel paint from the walls.

"Yeah," he said, giving me a short nod after he put the bottle down and took another slice of pizza. "Figure you're right. I got a long time to regret making the wrong choice. If he turns out to be an asshole, I can always change my mind, and it will be his loss, not mine. But if he's a decent guy..." He ended in a shrug. "Besides, it's not like I got much of anybody else now."

You've got me –

The words leaped to my lips, and I almost let them out.

But that was insane.

We barely knew each other, and if he decided not to stick around, then he wouldn't have me. Somebody had to stay here, had to be there for Clarion.

That somebody would be me if Reaper refused to step up.

"I don't think you'll regret it," I murmured.

Muscles shifted under smooth golden skin, mostly bared by the white tank he'd pulled on after we'd showered earlier. "We'll see." Slanting a look at me, he said, "Maybe you'll see about spilling whatever secrets you're holding onto now. Yeah?"

"Secrets?" My stomach twisted. Here I'd been thinking I was so good at hiding my reactions, my thoughts, my worries. But he'd seen something.

"Yeah. Secrets. You've got them in your eyes. I saw them on day one. When are you going to tell me whatever it is you've got to tell me'?"

Giving him a brilliant smile, I replied, "When I'm ready to. Besides, it's not really my secret."

10

Reaper

Clarion was a monster. The company, not the man.

Its headquarters were located in Cincinnati, but apparently, James – my *father* – had offices in Germany, Moscow, Mexico City and several other international locations, not to mention the manufacturing plants located in the US.

One of the largest securities firms in the world, they handled weapons and securities for both the public and private sectors, and word had it that they were in talks to become the lead distributor of firearms to the US military.

That was a BFD – big fucking deal.

I was familiar with several Clarion models and couldn't find any fault in them. Headquarters had several shooting ranges, a research and development lab, plus think tanks for all those experts in the field weapons.

Some might see Clarion as a place devoted to death.

In reality, Clarion was devoted to protecting life. Its security arm – developing armor, home intruder systems and other means of protecting self and home – were just as large and prolific as the weapons development.

"And they want to *sell* that part of the company off?" I asked, staring at the proposal in front of me. It looked like a bunch of foreign language, but there were a few things that made sense, and those were the numbers at the bottom.

They just didn't add up.

"What are your thoughts on it?" James asked.

"I think they need to go take a course in basic math," I said bluntly.

He broke out into a laugh.

It had been ten days since we'd had lunch – since O had come over and all but blown my mind in the backyard of my mother's house. The next day, I'd driven to the address she'd left for me and found James sitting down to a breakfast of oatmeal and grapefruit.

I told him it looked about as appetizing as it sounded, and he agreed.

"So why are you eating it?" I asked. "Your doctor said you've got three months. Eat whatever the hell you want."

O had given me a look like I was insane.

James had smiled. A few minutes later, he had a lavish plate of bacon, eggs, and waffles sitting in front of him, and his eyes were practically rolling into the back of his head.

I'd asked for the same.

Since then, we'd had dinner a few times, and we actually went fishing over the weekend at his stocked, private lake.

This week, he'd asked me if I'd enjoy taking a look around Clarion.

I'd almost said no, but he mentioned the new weapons they were developing. That sealed the deal.

"It does seem like they've forgotten the simple art of figuring out which number is bigger," James said, referring to the projected income losses I was looking at. His eyes narrowed. "The damn board is meeting to discuss this proposal in thirty minutes. I'd like you to come in and tell them that very thing."

"I...what?"

He lifted a shoulder and waved a hand around. "Come in and tell the board what you just said. It's time I introduced you anyway."

"Why?"

At that moment, O stepped into his office, carrying a slim file. She was dressed in a suit that almost looked like the clothes she would have worn before whatever transformation she'd undergone, save for a few small differences. The pants were fitted along her waist and hips before going looser and flowing down those long, long legs.

The white blouse had a rounded collar, almost school-girlish, giving it a feminine softness under the waist-length cropped jacket. She looked sexy and stylish and sharp.

Ten hours ago, she'd been pressed against the wall of the shower in my bathroom, moaning my name as I licked at the folds between her thighs, then crying out as I drove my dick into her.

As if sensing my thoughts, she looked at me, a faint blush on her cheeks.

"Hello, Adam."

"O." I studied her mouth for a long moment, just to see if I could get her to blush some more.

She did, and as she moved to stand behind James, she mouthed, *Stop it.*

I grinned.

"Will you be joining us, Adam?" James asked again, reminding me of our discussion.

It took a few seconds to recall what we'd been talking about.

The board meeting. Introducing me.

"Why do you want to introduce me?" I asked.

James canted his head to the side. "You're my son."

"And...that's got what to do with the board?"

O laid a hand on James's shoulder and held the file out to him.

He accepted it without even looking at her.

"As of yesterday, Adam, you've been named primary beneficiary in my will."

11

Reaper

I felt like I'd been sucker-punched. Maybe I shouldn't be so surprised.

Maybe I should have expected this.

But I felt like somebody had swung an ax at my head, and I'd just barely escaped with it still attached.

Even now, forty minutes into this meeting with the board members, sitting down at a long table, wearing a pair of khakis and a polo shirt, surrounded by a bunch of men in suits, I felt more out of place than I'd ever felt in my life.

I wanted a drink – badly.

I wanted to get up and get the hell out of there – badly.

O stood behind me, and at that moment, she brushed her fingers across my shoulder, almost like she could read my mind. If she could, I wouldn't be surprised.

These windbags were rambling on about how they could make so much more money and become so much more efficient if they focused all their energy on their primary moneymaker, and all I wanted to do was ask James what in the hell he was thinking.

He'd gone on to tell me that as his primary beneficiary, I'd inherit his stock in Clarion, and I'd take his place. O, of course, would be there to assist me in whatever capacity I needed. She had a ten-year contract with the company, and her position was secure. Only she could end the contract without serious financial compensation.

Not that I'd even consider getting rid of her.

Shit, you sound like you're considering doing this.

I couldn't do it.

There was no way.

But it wasn't like I had any control over what a man did with his will, did I? That didn't mean I had to accept it, though. If I didn't...

"James, old boy, I understand you've had some health issues, and maybe it's just because you've let O take on so much responsibility, but the facts are simply the facts."

That placating tone cut through the fog in my head, and I looked up to see a thin weasel of a man smiling at James. He gave O a smirking smile, one that seemed to say, *What does this twit know about what we do?*

Then he tapped the report in front of him. I had a copy of it too.

"Facts are facts," I heard myself saying. "You're damn right about that. And the fact of the matter is, you idiots sitting around this table here have forgotten basic math skills."

All eyes came to me. I hadn't spoken a word since I walked in, hadn't introduced myself or anything.

At first, people were curious, then they ignored me. Now I found myself the center of attention. Reaching out, I flipped to the pages where they broke down the numbers and started crunching them. "People can rig numbers and slant facts all they want. But some of these fees, the intake." I tapped the paper. "This is money you're *bleeding* – you're not making it." I shoved my paper across the table, the red and green marks I'd made the last few minutes standing out in stark contrast. "Now, maybe you all are used to those tricks like moving money from column A to column B and thinking that will hide the facts, but the bottom line is that you make just as much money up front with the home defense systems. Then, on top of that, there's the money that comes in from the monthly service that goes along with the home service. Easy money. You do little for it. You'd be an idiot to drop it."

I moved on to a few other things I'd noticed in the reports I'd read, watching as the weasel's face slowly went redder and redder.

Several times, one of them would try to interject and cut me off, but I just kept talking, using a calm, easy voice. Since they all seemed to want to hear what I had to say, they eventually went quiet.

Once I was done, the man who'd been seated in the chair directly across from James leaned forward, jabbing the air with the pen he held. "Mind telling me just who you are, son?"

"Don't call me son," I advised. I dismissed him and looked over at James, taking in once more the similarities between us – the eyes, the hair, the shape of his face and mine, our hands. Even the way we sat was almost identical. He'd done one tour in the military, only one, but that posture, the way he walked and sat and stood, it was something that tended to stay with a person. It wasn't just the posture though. There was no denying the physical similarities between us. Anybody who looked for it would see it.

He studied me with the same intense scrutiny that I directed at him, and I knew what he wanted.

"Well, *son*," the weasel curled his lip, "if you'd like me to call you by a name, perhaps you should provide one."

"Adam Dedman." I leveled a hard glare at him, and his eyes fell away from mine after less than a few seconds.

"And you're here because...?" The weasel hadn't lost his arrogant tone.

What a dumb-ass.

"Adam is here because I requested he join us," James said when I didn't respond. "Over the next few weeks, I'll be transferring the reins over to him – with Olivia at his side, of course."

None of them blinked.

They all just sat there, frozen, and for a few seconds, not a single one of them got it.

"Are you out of your fucking mind?" The weasel exploded from his chair and flung a hand toward me. "We don't even know who in the hell he is!"

"He's my son," James said in a quiet, polite voice.

It's strange, but I recognized that tone of voice. It was the same one I'd heard used by a few of my superiors when they were talking to truly stupid fools. The tone that somehow managed to silence all but the very, very moronic.

The weasel wasn't moronic.

His jaw snapped shut tightly, and he eased back, although he didn't return to his seat.

Seven sets of eyes came toward me. The only ones who weren't looking at me were O and James.

Pretending not to notice, I reached for my coffee and took a drink. It had started to cool, but we were getting ready to move into a series of psychological games, one headfuck after another. I didn't know shit about business, true. But I knew headfuck. The military was full of it.

A full thirty seconds passed before anyone spoke. A woman at the end of the table cleared her throat before breaking the silence. "Excuse me, James. I didn't know you had, um, another son."

I glanced her way.

"His mother and I were…estranged. And that's more than you're entitled to know."

I took another sip from my coffee, all the while keeping my eyes on the weasel. He wasn't looking at me. His attention was focused on James.

Save for the one moment when he glanced down the table.

I saw who he was looking at too.

The queen's sister. Cherise Whitney.

She noticed my attention before the weasel did, giving me a polite smile. Maybe if I hadn't spent too many years being trained to dig out the worst scum imaginable, I would have believed that polished façade.

But under that politeness, I saw something I was too familiar with.

Malice wore a lot of masks.

She turned her attention to James, looking for all the world like she was hanging onto every word he said.

When I looked back at him, the weasel was doing the same.

But I knew what I'd seen.

12

Olivia

"Honestly, I think they took it rather well." Standing in the boardroom while everybody drank their customary coffee and snacked on the light lunch James always provided, I studied the people around us.

Not that they'd know.

The reason James kept me handy was because I was good at doing all these little things without people realizing just what I was doing.

"You think that went well?" Reaper looked at me like I had lost my mind.

I grinned at the skepticism in his voice.

More than once, a couple of board members had all but exploded as they sat in their seats and listened to James lay down the law.

"You don't know these people. I do. The fact that most of them were cordial to you as we wrapped up is a good thing. I'd bet if we were in the middle of a cocktail party, they'd all be coming over to offer their congrats."

"They'd be coming over to slip arsenic into my glass."

"They might try." James joined us, studying me thoughtfully over the tops of his glasses. "I think we should do that."

"What...slip arsenic into his glass?" I cocked my head and looked over at Reaper. "Adam can be annoying, but I don't think I'm ready to poison him. Yet."

Reaper laughed. Even James cracked a smile, but he shook his head. "The cocktail party. Something to formally move him into his new position. Let's set it for the end of the week."

"Are you...what..." Reaper sputtered and finally managed to complete a sentence. A single, one word sentence. "No."

Both James and I ignored him as we focused on the particulars. "That sounds like a fine idea. Where should we have it?"

"The estate is too far out. Too many might use it as a reason to not come. That won't be acceptable." He coughed into his fisted hand, the fit lasting longer than I liked, and I pretended to occupy myself by making a few notes on my phone, although I heard every pained breath he tried to take. He was getting weaker, sicker. He wasn't even taking chemo.

I knew he had spoken to the queen about his diagnosis. They were holding on for each other now. I imagined as soon as one passed, the other would follow within days, if not hours.

My heart started to ache, and I shoved it aside.

I couldn't afford to hurt right now.

I'd have to hold everything up until Reaper could do it on his own.

"I'm leaving you the house."

I dropped my phone.

Tears blurred my eyes, and I whispered, "Damn you. Don't do this to me. Not right now."

He laid a hand on my shoulder while Reaper knelt and picked up my phone. Distantly, I noticed that he had taken a few steps, placing his solid body between me and the others still milling around the wide, airy room, providing me with the illusion of privacy.

"O."

"Olivia," I snapped at him, jerking my head up to glare at the man who hadn't just been a *father*. He'd been my teacher, my friend. Everything I had could be traced back to that one act of kindness years ago. "You...you never call me O."

The hand resting on my shoulder slid around until he

could pull me into a quick, casual hug. It was all I'd accept, considering where we were, and he knew it. He let me go in an instant.

"It shouldn't go to me," I said stiltedly.

James started to respond, but Reaper beat him to it.

"Don't start that shit." He turned and stared at me. "You're more his kid than I am. The house, this place..." He waved a hand. "I don't even know why I'm *here*. But if he wants to leave you the house, this place, the whole jalopy, I can't fault him for it."

Then shrugging, clearly uncomfortable, Reaper demanded, "What about this stupid party?"

∽

THE LAST THING I should be doing when I had a big party to plan was make the forty-five-minute drive to the little cottage styled house in the Cincinnati suburbs where I knew I'd find one Adam Dedman.

But that's what I found myself doing at half past eleven that night, the top on my Mercedes-Benz down so the wind was tearing through my hair...and drying the tears on my face.

James was dying.

He was already getting weaker and sicker.

In fact, it had been happening for a while, and I'd just refused to let myself see it. It was like having Reaper appear had made it...okay for me to accept the inevitable.

"It's not," I told myself. "It's *not*."

I hit the steering wheel with my balled up fist and resisted, barely, the urge to scream.

I wanted to scream, to rant, to rail at the injustice of it all, but I didn't.

Taking the turn into the subdivision at a speed that sent the tires to squealing, I tore down the road and slammed on the brakes so hard, I ended up slamming forward. Only the seatbelt kept me from hitting the steering wheel.

I pulled the keys out, staring at the darkened lights.

What if Adam wasn't home?

What if–

The lights came on.

I didn't even remember climbing out of the car or starting up the sidewalk.

One minute I was in the car.

Then I was in front of him.

"O?"

He wore a pair of low-slung sweats, leaving his chest and abdomen bare. He'd lost weight, his hip bones pronounced. Every muscle was defined and hard, and the despair inside me morphed into something else. Something that had an outlet.

I lunged for him.

He caught me, and when his mouth slammed down on mine, I had to wonder if maybe he'd been waiting for me. Hoping for me.

I practically climbed up his body, wrapping my legs around his hips. Big, hard hands caught my ass and held me up as he boosted me higher. "Hold on," he muttered, breaking the kiss just long enough to say those two words.

Hold on...to what? Him?

He was the only thing that felt solid and real, so I'd do that. I'd hold on to him.

The earth spun, shook...he was walking.

Then my feet were on the floor, and he'd stopped kissing me. "Hey," I grumbled.

"You're overdressed," he said, gripping the loose material of the sundress I'd pulled on.

It was the *only* thing I'd pulled on, and judging by the look on his face, he hadn't been expecting that.

I brought my hands up instinctively, but he caught them. Looking around, I realized he'd brought us into his living room, and I let him guide my hands back down.

"I love your body, O," he said, dipping his head to press a kiss to the upper slope of my left breast, then my right. "You're about the sexiest thing I've ever seen."

"You need to get out more." I wasn't trying to take a dig at myself. I wasn't unattractive. I had my strong points, but I also knew I wasn't in the same league as some the women around here.

"No." He caught my face in his hands and arched my chin

up until we were staring into each other's eyes.

"You..." He kissed one cheekbone.

"Are..." He kissed the other cheekbone.

"So..." His mouth grazed mine, and I shivered.

"Fucking..." He bit my lower lip and tugged.

"Sexy." He caught my naked hips and pulled me in close, until the only thing that separated us where the sweats he wore. "It hurts just to look at you."

I whimpered because now *I* was hurting. I could feel the heat and hardness of him, and I wanted him inside me. *Bad.*

"Feel me." His voice was a growl. Catching my hand, he guided me until my fingers were fisted around his cock. "Feel what you do..."

Up, down...he pulsed against my touch. When he let go, I dipped my hand inside his sweats.

Dimly, I knew that he'd braced both of his hands on the door over my head. He'd carried me inside, shut the door and put my back against it. That was it. Now, as I stood there naked, I began to stroke him. His baggy pants were in the way, so I used my free hand to tug them down.

He pulled back, and I made a frustrated noise.

"So impatient," he said when he came back to me.

I went to take his cock in my hand again, but he stopped me, picking me up.

"Adam..."

"Olivia..."

He guided my legs around his hips and I shivered, whimpering a little as I felt the head of his cock teasing my folds. I was so wet already, and the hard steel of his cock made me shiver. "In me...now," I demanded.

"Bossy. I love that in a woman." He teased me more, though, passing over me once, twice...

I slammed my head back against the door and groaned, twisting my hips, trying to guide him home.

"You keep that up, and I'm going to go a little crazy."

"I'm way past that point. Stop teasing me. Just fuck me."

"I'll do more than that," he promised. Then he drove inside.

I screamed. He buried himself all the way to the root in one long driving thrust, and I was still struggling to adjust when he did it a second time, then a third.

"Look at me," he said, voice raw and harsh. One big hand cupped my face, his thumb lifting my chin. "Look at me..."

His eyes, hot and burning and so dark, all but consumed me. When his mouth took mine, I knew I *had* been consumed. Taken over. By him.

He drove a climax from me, then another.

I was shaking and almost ready to beg for mercy when he caught my ass in his hands and slowed his thrusts, shifting around until his back was to his door. Then he began to lift me, dragging me up and down his swollen length as he watched me. "You're getting inside my soul, O," he said. "All the way in..."

I groaned, my head falling back.

I felt every nuance of him as he continued to guide the slow, almost torturous rhythm, each stroke, each movement designed to incite madness inside me.

"Now," he said, his cock swelling. "Come...I can feel that snug cunt getting hot and tight again. Come..."

I exploded.

This time, so did he.

~

"You know you can't run from this."

Reaper lay against my back, one hand on my belly.

We'd taken a shower, and he'd taken me...again. Slowly, this time, starting with him going down on me and ending with him turning me away while he slid in from behind, bringing me to a sweet, nearly endless climax.

But it didn't end there.

We'd come to his room, and there, he stretched me out on my belly, massaged my back, my legs and arms...then he turned me over, put my knees up to my ears and pounded into me until I was breathless.

Now, sticky from him and sweat and needing another shower, I'd been *this* close to sleeping.

And he wanted to talk.

"I wasn't running from anything," I said sullenly. "I was

horny, and I wanted sex."

He was quiet for so long, I didn't think he'd respond.

"Okay then." He kissed my shoulder.

He was going to let it go. Part of me was mad. I needed to talk. He was supposed to push me. That's what couples–

"What are we?" I asked, my voice shaking.

That's what couples did...

I was acting like we were involved. All we'd had was sex – excellent sex, but it was sex. Did he even care?

"What are we?"

He shifted on the bed, and I squeezed my eyes closed. Here we go. I'd done it now. I'd broached the relationship thing, and he was going to get up, leave – no, wait. He was going to throw me out. Then he'd avoid me, and things would be awkward and...

He rolled, pulling me with him and moving around until he was on his back, and I was sprawled against his chest.

"I never thanked you for helping me out when I screwed things up – being there, bailing me out." He waited a beat, then said, "Thanks. It's a weird way to start a relationship. Then I disappeared and tried to drown myself in a bottle...even worse. But...well, that's how things go sometimes."

I blinked down at him, not quite following.

He grinned up at me. "This is where you offer something. *Yes, Reaper...I want to be involved in a relationship with you,*" he said, his voice rising in a pitiful imitation of a woman.

"Yes, Reaper," I said, feeling a little off-balance. "I want to be in a relationship – wait. Are you talking like friends with benefits?"

He stroked his knuckles down my back. The caress made me shiver. "I've got friends. Some good ones, and I've been an asshole to them. Still, I've got some friends. The idea of being friends with you...benefits or not...no. That's not what I want. Or at least not all."

The warm, sweet emotion that bloomed in my chest was one I hadn't ever experienced before. I savored it, every bit of it, as I lowered my head and kissed him. "Adam, I'd like to be in a relationship with you. Of course, it will be complicated. You're kind of like, um, my boss now. Although I know way more than you do."

"Sounds a lot like how things have been with a lot of my bosses. Although I've never wanted to bend any of them over the nearest desk and screw them silly." He grinned at me. But the smile faded, and he reached up, brushed my hair back. "You still going to pretend you're not running, O?"

To my horror, tears began to burn my eyes.

I dropped my head down onto his chest and started to weep.

"I'm not ready to lose him, Reaper."

He held me.

He kissed my hair.

And in the quiet of the night, he said, "I know, O. I know."

13

Reaper

The glitz and glam and sparkles were going to blind me.

I felt entirely out of place.

I was almost certain that there were women here at my party wearing shoes that cost more than I used to make in a month – no, I was certain. Before the party, O had insisted we go shopping, and she'd picked out several outfits for me. The price tags there had left me speechless.

Technically, I knew that some people spent that kind of money but seeing it in action left me shaking my head. Then she'd insisted I get fitted for a custom tux. *Not for the party. It's dressy casual, but you need a tux for the formal functions.*

I didn't see why anybody required a penguin suit, but what the hell.

"Well, look at you."

The familiar voice had me grinning, and I turned. Ignoring the hand that was offered, I grabbed Hawk and hauled him in for a hug. "Man, it's good to see you."

"You clean up nice." He looked at me in the clothes O had helped me select – purchased on an account that she had set up. *Your account, of course.* Then she'd gone with me to the bank so we could take care of a few small issues. Small. To the tune of a bank balance that had left me feeling light-headed.

James Clarion, my father, was a fucking billionaire and then some.

And I was about to inherit it.

The *why* and *how* of it all made me a little sick.

"So...I'm here at this party because you're being made CEO of Clarion Arms and Securities," Hawk said, settling into the empty space next to me.

"Um..." I rubbed at my neck, trying to figure out the best way to explain the insane change in my circumstances. "Yeah. Turns out he's kinda...well. He's my father."

Hawk gave me a long, intense study and then went back to watching the crowd. "Should figure that you'd find a way to come out of everything on your feet, kid."

With a disgusted sound, I shook my head. "I don't know how to handle all of this."

Across the room, I caught the sound of O's laugh, and I followed it, finding myself staring at her.

She was dressed in red. The dress wrapped around her, crisscrossing at her breasts and hips, emphasizing her curves and making her excellent legs look endless. Hawk followed my gaze and made a low hum under his breath. "I'm assuming you can handle her just fine."

"Actually..." I shot him a look.

He arched his brows and then a grin broke out over his face. "Well, hell, man. You went and took the fall, didn't you?"

I shoved him lightly but went back to staring at O.

If James hadn't approached us at that moment, I might have embarrassed myself, because she really did look amazing in that dress.

"Adam."

I nodded at him, trying to brush off the concern I felt. He looked even more tired, grayer, older now than he did two days ago. He told O he'd start coming into the office only two days a week now, but I wondered how long that would last.

"Hey." I nodded at him before gesturing to Hawk and making the introductions. It didn't take long before Hawk segued into a discussion about some of the newer models Clarion had on the market.

James looked like he'd found his new best friend.

"It's nice to see you two bonding," I said, amused.

They ignored me, and I shook my head, wandering off.

O had disappeared a few minutes ago. I'd seen the direction she'd gone and thought I'd try to find her. Just for a few minutes in private. We had a date for tomorrow, a real date, our first one.

But if I didn't get another taste of that mouth...

She'd been moving toward the hedge maze located in the main grounds, so that was my direction as well. As I neared the entrance to the maze, I looked for the security guard who was supposed to be standing at this location.

He wasn't there.

Slowing my pace, I looked around. An alarm began to whisper in my head. It wasn't a loud one. Too many things that were loud ended up with the bad side effect of death and destruction.

There should be *several* guards around the grounds. I'd met the entire team and knew that Sullivan was supposed to be here. He was a nice guy, older, former army. A cop who picked up extra money on weekends doing security detail. The decent, responsible sort. Not somebody who'd walk off because he had to take a piss less than an hour into the event.

Hearing footsteps behind me, I ducked into the maze and twisted around the very first turn. I don't know what propelled me to do that. A moment later, a foot scuffed up against the stone where Sullivan should have been.

"All is secure on this end, over."

Secure...over.

Somebody was sending out a status update.

There was a pause, followed by, "No sir. Nobody saw – I'm absolutely positive. Yes, he's neutralized. Over."

Neutralized?

Angling my head around, I followed the sound of the voice, pinpointing the speaker's location better. I caught a glimpse of him. He was close to the entrance, taking the place of the hired guard. He was wearing a tactical uniform.

Had Sullivan been *neutralized*?

I set my jaw as more voices and noise began to draw closer. I needed to be somewhere else. Actually, I needed to know what the fuck was going on, but I wasn't going to get that information getting caught.

The hedge had any number of dips and natural camouflage, and I took advantage of every bit of it as I eased away from as much of the noise as I could while still staying close to the first person I'd heard speaking.

The man clearly didn't do stealth all that much.

He wore too much deodorant for it. He still smelled like body odor and sweat, thickly veiled under a heavy dousing of Axe body spray.

He continued to have a one-way conversation, and I would have killed to have access to some of my old equipment. Since that wasn't going to happen…

He signed off on the call, and I came out behind him, wrapping a forearm around his neck, jerking upward.

He was big, strong, and fast.

But he wasn't prepared to deal with somebody like me.

I had him neutralized in seconds and dragged him into the hedge, shoving him not too gently into the greenery after I took a minute to strip off anything useful to cuff his hands behind his back. He had a roll of duct tape fastened to a hoop on his tactical vest. I cut a piece off, slapping it over his mouth as I listened.

More voices.

And there was one coming over the phone.

Shoving his Bluetooth into my ear, I melted back into the shadows just as somebody came around the corner, his weapon up and ready, looking around.

Over the Bluetooth, I heard an insistent voice.

"Is the entrance secure? She's coming. We don't have time for fuck-ups!"

She…

Who?

But my gut was already screaming.

"Tiger One, report."

I had a feeling Tiger One was snoozing away in dreamland in the hedge behind me. I kept the silenced Beretta ready as I ducked into what turned out to be a dead end – but that was fine. I needed back-up.

I pulled out my phone and used my body to hide the screen as I dimmed the screen down to nothing. I sent a quick text to Hawk.

His response was fast.

You've got to be shitting me.

I DIDN'T BOTHER RESPONDING, just punched in what facts I had. They were pitifully few.

His next response was a lot more in line with what I needed.

Son of a bitch. You find trouble everywhere. On my way.

Not bothering to reply, I silenced the phone and shoved it into my back pocket. Then I cleared the narrow path that had led me to the dead end.

Then I focused on another, and another, following the sound of the voices coming from somewhere inside the maze.

Finally, they became clearer, and worse, vaguely familiar.

"This isn't right...not the way..." a man was saying, his nasally tone coming in harsh whispers.

"We've already agreed," a female voice hissed. "You're in this as much as I am."

They argued back and forth, their voices dipping too low for me to hear them at times. Finally, the man cursed and nearly yelled, "We'll find another way to get it done."

I placed him.

The weasel.

Russel Braxton – the board member who'd been so pissed off earlier in the week when James had announced the changes coming down the pipeline for Clarion.

And the woman...I almost had her voice placed.

But then another voice rang out from the entrance. "Okay, Russel. Where are you?"

My skin went icy, dread crawling up my spine.

O.

I started moving quicker, faster, moving to intersect.

"Call him," the woman hissed.

My phone vibrated a second later, but I ignored it as I peered through the gap in the hedges, staring in. I could just barely make out O, that murder red dress. The others, though...I couldn't see them for shit. Didn't know what weapons they possessed or who else they had with them.

My phone vibrated again.

"He's not answering," Russel said, his voice panicked. "Look, Cherise, let's–"

The woman interrupted him, her voice coming out too loud and fast. "Olivia. Hello, we've been..."

Cherise.

Olivia.

"Okay, big guy...I think you've heard enough," a calm voice said, right before I felt the muzzle of a gun pressed against the back of my skull.

SEALionaire Book 3

1

Olivia

Seeing Cherise and Russel Harris together didn't exactly do wonderful things for my mood or my sanity, but I didn't have time to deal with their bullshit tonight. James needed me.

He was getting tired too easily these days.

An ache tried to settle in my throat, but I shoved it aside. I could cry and get maudlin and sad later, when I wasn't dealing with a cutthroat bitch and her flying monkey.

Or witch...

I smirked, amusing myself as I pictured Cherise a lovely shade of green.

The smile faded, and fast, as she lifted a hand from her side.

"It's time to be done with you, darling," she said.

I recognized the gun. It was a Clarion CR12, similar to the Glock 19. It was too big for her hand, but she didn't seem fazed by that fact.

"You know, if you want to get more involved in the tactical side of Clarion Arms, I can help. That pistol is too big for you." I kept my voice neutral as I slowly lifted my eyes to hers. "We have smaller handguns. You even talked about how cute they were at the board meeting last year, remember?"

"Yes." She flashed a toothy smile at me. "And you shot down the idea of creating a designer line."

"Weapons aren't toys," I said flatly. "They don't need to look like them."

She waved what certainly wasn't a toy at me. "Oh, never mind that. That's far from my concern now, but I'll get back to that idea sooner or later...once I'm in control."

"You?" I fought the urge to laugh. "James would sooner leave Clarion in the hands of a gorilla than you. The gorilla has more sense."

Tiny lines fanned out from her eyes, but the anger I'd hoped to incite didn't rouse. Damn it. Sweat beaded along the back of my neck, slid down the inside of my dress.

"Do shut up, Olivia. You've been a pain in the ass since day one."

"The feeling is mutual." I heard noises and was vaguely aware that there were others in the small clearing near the center of the maze. But I didn't dare look away from her – or the Clarion CR12. "You do realize that I'm not the real problem, right? James has named his son as the one who'll take over, and the cops will look long and hard at everybody on the board if something happens to him."

"Oh, something *will*." She laughed brightly. "He's going to jail for *killing* you, Olivia. He's already gotten himself into so much trouble. That was considerate of him to sow the seeds there."

"Killing..." I licked my lips, fought to keep my teeth from chattering. "You plan on killing me and framing him?"

The gun didn't so much as tremble. "You are quite bright. We just need him to get here."

"You're insane. And you're an idiot." Terror had my heart pounding like a mad thing, but I struggled to stay in control. I had to think. I didn't believe for a second that what she was saying would work, but personally, I was fond of life and knew better than to rely on hope as a strategy.

"We have witnesses, darling."

Off to the side, I heard a low grunt, a noise. Too low for them to hear. Cherise didn't look away from my face, but she did speak to Russel. "Where *is* he? We need him here for this to work."

"I've already tried calling him several times. I texted him and said it was urgent – an emergency," Russel said, his voice a near whine.

"Go *get* him," Cherise hissed. "You need this as much as I do, remember?"

As he backed away, I shot a look at his face, but he was too busy staring at his feet. I sucked in a breath, swinging my gaze back to Cherise. If I screamed, would anybody hear?

The party was loud, and the house was too far away.

"Hillsworth," Cherise said softly just as a twig snapped beside me.

A shadow separated itself from the hedges and came to stand in front of me.

The man was big, so big he all but blotted out the carefully placed lights that dotted the hedge maze.

The sight of the gun in Cherise's hand had scared me, yes. Terrified me, even.

But the sight of this man did more than terrify me. His eyes were dead. Cold and dead. A few seconds ago, I'd been methodically thinking about what I needed to do to survive – and I hadn't really even *doubted* it. I mean, Cherise trying to kill me? She was malicious enough, I didn't question that. But she was also afraid of spiders and mice and blood. An assistant had cut a finger once, and she'd all but passed out.

I could handle somebody who got weak-kneed at the sight of blood.

This man probably finger-painted with it.

Everything in me screamed to back up and run, but common sense told me to be smart. You didn't run from predators.

So even when he took a step closer, I didn't let myself back up. I slowed my breathing and paid attention to everything. Watched. Listened. His muscles tensed just a fraction of a second before he moved.

I dropped, but it was only barely in time.

Kicking my shoes off would have saved a few seconds, but I hadn't exactly come back here expecting to have somebody point a gun at my face or send a goon after me. Fortunately, I'd grown up living a life that prepared me for a lot of things, and I knew how to use everything to my advantage. A split second after I dropped, the shoes were off. I grabbed one of them and flipped it in my palm. As he bent to grab me, I drove the heel into his calf. Most shoe heels would have broken. My shoes were custom made and not just for looks.

James hadn't just hired me to be his problem solver.

The first time he'd taken me to London, I'd gone as his assistant, and we'd been jumped in the parking garage. The policeman had stated in very cute, very crisp British tones that if I ever wanted a job, to just look him up. The two men had been on the ground, one moaning, his knee busted. The other had been red-faced and still struggling to breathe after I all but crushed his larynx.

Of course, my official title said nothing about the fact that I often acted as a bodyguard. All the extra training paid off, for now at least. I hit him with enough force to hurt before slamming my fist into his knee.

It buckled, and he toppled, swearing furiously.

I was still alive.

That was a good thing.

And I didn't know how long that good thing would last.

The big bastard had a weapon of his own, and I knew he'd be faster, smarter than Cherise. I hadn't broken his knee. He was already upright, and now he was pissed.

Slowly backing away from him, I weighed my options.

"Don't make this any harder than it has to be," the big guy said.

Hillsworth. She'd called him Hillsworth.

"Oh, I'm going to make it plenty hard." They had no *idea* how hard I planned on making things.

"Would you just *get* her and shut her up?" Cherise demanded, her voice a harsh whisper.

Russel was looking around awkwardly, and if I didn't know better, I'd think he looked guilty. Bastard. Son of a bitch. He *should* look guilty. He'd called me, told me to come here – set me up.

"It won't work," I said, lying through my teeth. "You need Adam here, right? Well, he headed out right as I was coming over here. Saw an old friend of his and they were going to go grab a drink or two. This...socializing thing isn't his milieu."

The man in front of me didn't pay attention to a single word I said. Russel squawked though. "See? We need to just call this off. It won't work. You heard her."

"She's lying," Cherise said.

But I could feel her watching me, looking for some sign to assure herself that she was right. She wasn't going to find one. I could lie far too well, even for my own comfort.

Lifting a shoulder, I said, "Apparently you didn't see how uncomfortable he was. When he ran into his friend, he practically leaped at the chance to blow this joint." For added effect, I muttered, "Asshole."

That caught Cherise's attention.

As I eased back a few more inches, Hillsworth took another step toward me. I was more than a little pleased to see he was limping.

"Hillsworth?" she asked, the question in her voice obvious.

"We'll take her alive, wait for him. We can still make it work," he said, a slow smile curling his lips. "I told you there might be a need to improvise. The price will go up."

The dick was standing there talking about killing me the same way some people might discuss buying a car.

Swallowing, I backed up a bit more.

I was almost to the gap in the hedges. I knew this maze. I'd spent a lot of time in this garden.

I could run.

Almost there...

He lunged.

2

Reaper

Disabling the prick who'd pulled a gun on me took a little longer than I would have liked.

It had only been a split second, but that split second was keeping me from O.

The thug lay on the ground, eyes blank, his face slack as he stared sightlessly off to the side. His neck was broken. Since he wouldn't be needing the Glock 19 he'd been carrying, I helped myself to it.

Two guns. Nothing to put either one in, but that was the least of my problems.

A noise had me lifting the weapon I held in my right hand, a silenced Beretta.

"Dial it back," Hawk whispered as he emerged from the night, his eyes narrowed to slits as he studied the dead body. "Passed one on my way in. Figured I'd go ahead and address the situation."

I took that to mean he'd either knocked out or killed the son of a bitch.

Turning over the Glock, I updated him on what I knew, which was just a little above next to nothing.

He checked the weapon as I summarized the situation. Then we moved back to my previous location. I could still hear the murmured voices, and as we drew a little closer, I could see flashes of color through breaks in the hedge too. Not much. The red of O's dress and something pale and glittery. Another woman. Cherise.

As I listened to them talk, my blood ran cold.

My muscles tensed, the urge to rush out there stronger than I liked.

Rushing into things wasn't just an amateur's mistake – it was an idiot's. Maybe I'd done some idiotic things in my life, but I don't consider myself an idiot as a whole. But it was hell, crouching there in the dark and listening as a cold, emotionless voice said, "We'll take her alive, wait for him. We can still make it work. I told you there might be a need to improvise. The price will go up."

You have no idea what the price is going to be, you miserable fuck.

I could barely seem him, but their footsteps were getting closer.

I shot a look at Hawk.

His lean, dark face was tight, intense.

I looked back at the gap as a shadow fell long across it.

The only warning I had was that flash of red.

I grabbed her and spun to the side, trusting Hawk to have my back.

There was a struggle behind me, but for a second, I had my hands full. O slammed her head back, snarling and fighting like a demon. Her heel came down on my foot at the same time her head smacked into my nose.

"Damn it!"

Spinning her around, I pinned her up against me as blood started to pour. I tasted it in the back of my mouth. "It's me, O. It's Reaper. Adam."

"Reaper...Adam...." Her eyes widened, and she looked around. "Cherise...she's got a gun."

Son of a bitch.

"Stay!" I barked at her and hoped like hell she'd listen as I pressed back up against the hedge. Hawk and the bastard who'd threatened O were grappling, but it was already leaning heavily in Hawk's direction. The man had some serious skills though. Part of me was already frozen with the knowledge of what could have happened to O.

A wild shot had me crouching close to the ground.

"Cherise?"

Off to the side, a bright glare caught my eye. A cell phone. I didn't dare look over to see what O was doing, but I'd bet my left nut she was calling the cops.

"You might as well stop this bullshit right now," I said, trying for a pragmatic approach. "The cops are already on their way, and they've been given your name."

"I...Cherise, it's over."

My ears cataloged the voice, processed, recognized then filed the speaker away. Russel. The weasel from the board. Not a problem. Even if I hadn't met him, I'd know he wasn't my problem. His voice was quivery and broken, like he was struggling to hold it together.

"Come on, Cherise. Just put the gun down and we can—"

The words ended abruptly, cut off by another shot. But I doubted that one was quite as wild.

I chanced another look around the hedge. Cherise stood there, almost as if the moment had been crafted by an artist, wearing a pale dress that shimmered in the light, the moon shining down on her as she studied something on the ground.

No.

Not something.

A man – possibly a dead one.

Russel, if I had to make a bet.

She lifted her head.

Our eyes met.

The weapon she held came up.

It was a big pistol, too big for her, but she was compensating by using two hands to steady it.

It was dark, but if I had to make a guess, I'd say I was staring at a CR12 – Clarion's answer to the Glock M17. Whether or not she could make a shot at this distance was up in the air, but I was thinking not. Her hands were shaking from the weight of the gun already, and her eyes looked half-wild.

However, the weapon would do a decent amount of damage, and I'd rather not get shot by some crazy woman with a vendetta.

"You don't want to do this," I said, glancing around to find Hawk pulling the other dude behind a large bush.

"The hell I don't." She glared at me, lips trembling, eyes glittering. "You fucked up *everything*. Do you get that? *Everything!*"

"Yeah, I'm good at that." Nodding toward the weapon, I said, "You'll never come close with that, heavy as it is, far away as I am. Why don't you go ahead and lower it?"

"Why don't you kiss my ass?" She sneered at me, her eyes wild as she swept a quick look around.

Too quick.

She hadn't seen my weapon yet, and while I could take her out easy enough, I didn't want to kill her if I didn't have to. Of course, the fact that she was holding a gun on me wasn't really weighing in her favor.

"I can take the shot," Hawk said, his voice low.

I gave a small shake of my head. "Come on, Cherise. Just lower your weapon. You heard Russel. It's over. Cops are on their way. You're in enough trouble."

"Me?" She laughed, the noise half-hysterical. "I didn't do anything. You..." She licked her lips and nodded. "I'm protecting myself. The two of you...yes. You two were out to get me."

Well, I had to give her credit. She was definitely not willing to go down.

"And the men you hired? What's their story?"

She blinked, looking almost child-like. "What men?"

"My friend has one restrained on the ground behind me. I left one hog-tied and gagged in the hedge. The other one is dead." I kept my eyes on the weapon. "What do you think they'll tell the police?"

Her mouth opened and closed soundlessly.

Then Cherise turned the gun toward herself.

"No!" The shriek came from O.

She started to dart around me, and I caught her around the waist when she would have rushed out there.

Cherise's eyes lit up. Hell. I should have taken the shot, I realized.

She turned the weapon, her hands much steadier than I

would have thought she was capable of, the weapon pointed at both of us.

The crack that went through the air stole the air out of me.

Even when Cherise crumpled, blood blossoming like an ugly rose across the front of her pale dress, I still had a hard time breathing.

O stood frozen in my arms.

It could only have been seconds. In reality, I knew that. But it felt like a lifetime before either of us so much as moved.

Then I was running my hands over her, checking for injuries that didn't exist, shaking her and shouting. "I told you to stay, damn it! Why didn't you stay?"

"I'm not a dog, you son of a bitch!" she shouted back even as her hands patted my shirt. "Are you hurt? Did she shoot you?"

I didn't bother to answer that, hauling her up against me and sealing my mouth over hers.

O.

That was all I could think.

O.

She was here.

She was safe.

They hadn't hurt her.

"Ouch!" I jerked my head back, my tongue throbbing. She'd bitten me. And not in that fun, *I can't wait to get naked* way either.

She pulled away. "We can't do this," she said, shaking her head. "Not now. Not here."

I stared at her back as she walked away on shaky legs straight toward Cherise. Hawk was already there, the gun Cherise had been holding securely under his foot.

I wanted to haul her back against me and kiss her again. Bite her – in that sexy, *I can't wait to get you naked* way.

But she was right.

We couldn't do this here. Or now.

Voices were calling for us.

And the music had been cut off.

Sirens were blaring instead.

Sirens.

Shit.

"They'll pull through."

James sat across from us, his face gray with exhaustion.

He'd just disconnected from a call with somebody at the hospital. I don't know who he'd spoken with, but he had information on Cherise – and Russel.

Russel was in surgery, but he was lucky to still be alive.

Cherise had been lucky too. Hawk hadn't shot to kill.

The two men Hawk and I had dealt with had been turned over to the police, and at least one of them was already talking, and talking fast.

The dead body…well, the cops weren't too happy about that one, and I had already explained multiple times that the bastard had held a gun to my head.

"If he had a gun to your head, how come he's the one who's dead?" they kept asking.

And I kept looking at them like they were idiots. "He's dead because he had a gun to my head. What was I going to do…ask him nicely to not do that shit again?"

Eventually, somebody had come up and whispered something in the detective's ear, and he grunted, walked off to talk to another detective, both of them staring at me hard.

Since I hadn't been told not to, I'd walked off to find O.

That was over an hour ago, and she still wasn't looking at me.

Her sexy red dress was ruined, streaked with dirt and blood.

There was a scratch on her cheek and more smudges of dirt, her normally sleek hair disheveled. Her eyes were red, and I could tell she hadn't always managed to hold the tears back.

"What will happen to her?" O asked, her attention focused on Cherise.

I wanted to ask what the hell it mattered. She'd conspired to kill O. The woman should rot in jail. Granted, she'd done a miserable job of conspiring to kill O, but she didn't deserve to be rewarded for her failure by *not* doing time.

"We'll figure that out later." James patted her hand.

"This is going to break the queen's heart," O said.

The hoarseness in her voice hit me in the gut, and I realized suddenly why she'd rushed out when it looked like Cherise might kill herself. It was because of Elise. The woman O thought of as her own mother.

Baby...

Unable to stay away any longer, I went to the small sofa and sat down next to her. She stiffened but didn't pull away. "Something tells me your queen is made of sterner stuff than that." I stroked a hand down her back and leaned in to rest my chin on her head.

She turned her face into my chest, a shaky sigh escaping her.

Reaction slid over me, and I locked it down. I could have lost her.

I was just starting to realize what I'd found, and I'd come this close to losing her.

Another shaky sigh.

"I think I'll take myself off to bed," James murmured.

O didn't seem to notice.

James met my eyes. "Both of you should rest as well. Tomorrow..." He shook his head and looked at his watch. "Well, today will come soon enough."

I'd already noticed the time.

It was pushing two in the morning.

We'd have to be up and deal with the fall-out from this.

"Yeah."

I had a room where I could sleep, assuming I could.

O had a room of her own as well.

The party had been held at an old, elegant home perched on the banks of the Ohio. Once a private home, the place was now rented out for parties and stuff – and the entire house could be included in the package.

That was what O had arranged, knowing James would be too tired after the party for the drive home.

I hadn't planned on staying.

But now...

She shifted against me again, and this time, when she made that soft, gasping little breath, it was almost like a sob.

I pulled her onto my lap and kissed her cheek. "Don't cry."

"I'm not."

I could taste her tears. "Good." I kissed them away and said it again, "Don't cry."

She curled her arms around my neck and cuddled in closer. "I'm not crying."

She pressed her mouth to mine, and the steely grip I'd had around my control crumbled to dust. She was definitely not crying.

Surging upright, holding O clamped against me, we left the room. Her bedroom was upstairs and too far away. Mine was down here on the lower left, in the...west wing? Left wing? Whichever one, too far.

We ended up in another bedroom, one that had been set aside in case anybody over did it with the free booze and needed to sleep it off. Nobody had needed the room, which was good because I might have kicked them out.

Half stumbling into the room, I tossed O onto the bed and came down on her, desperation all but burning me alive.

I felt like if I didn't get my hands on her, if we weren't touching, skin to skin, within the next few seconds, something devastating would happen.

"You sure you're okay?" I asked as I studied her eyes.

She held my gaze. "Please...make me forget."

Grabbing the hem of her dress, I worked it up as I caught her lower lip and tugged, licked, bit...

She moaned against my mouth, her hands kneading my waist.

I broke away to peel the dress off her, tossing it into the corner. I wanted to burn the damn thing. It was filthy, ruined, a reminder of what could have happened. Focusing back on her, I levered my weight back up and settled on my heels, looking down at her.

The strapless black bra and panties gleamed against pale, smooth skin. That skin was marred with bruises now, and when I eased my hands down her thighs, she winced at the touch of my left thumb on her knees.

The torn, discolored flesh enraged me. But I throttled it down and shifted until I could bend and press my mouth to the unmarred skin just above the small injury. There were other marks, other bruises.

But she was whole. It could have been so much worse.

Moving my mouth higher, I traced the edge of her panties. O pushed her hands into my hair. "Please," she whispered.

I nuzzled her through the silk. She was already wet.

The light caress had her arching up, pushing herself against me, demanding more and I took that demand – happily. Through the material, I licked and touched and when she went to shove her panties down, swearing in frustration, I caught her wrists, pinning them to the bed by her hips.

"Not yet," I said roughly. "Once I get you naked, it's all over."

"Adam, please."

But I continued, stroking her lightly through her clothing. My cock was iron-hard, and the thought of feeling her wet cunt around me had my balls drawing tight. She jerked against the hold I had on her wrists. "If you don't fuck me right now," she said, voice breaking, "I'll...I swear I'll..."

Her clit was a hard bud, stiff, and even through her panties, I could feel it pulsing. With slow, deliberate pressure, I scraped my teeth over it.

O's cry broke over me – and she broke under me, shaking and shuddering, jerking against my hands as she rocked her hips feverishly. Her climax was the end of me. Shoving upright, I grabbed her panties and jerked at them. They didn't peel away as easily as I wanted so I just tore them off. If my damn trousers would have cooperated, I would have torn them off as well, but they were more resistant, and I had to wait long enough to shove them down.

She was still gasping, her body shuddering from the climax when I grabbed her left knee, hooked it over my elbow, opening her fully.

I thrust in, past the tight resistance of her pussy, gritting my teeth as she milked me, clenching around me like a fist. Her eyes went blind, and I felt it, another orgasm building inside her.

I withdrew slightly, feeling the drag of her tissues rasping over me and it was one the best damn things I'd ever felt in my life. But not enough. She fisted her hands against my chest, shoving against me slightly, her eyes wide, mouth open as she gasped for air.

I kissed her, stealing that breath into myself as I worked

deeper and deeper into her cunt.

A moan shimmered out of her on the next thrust, while those intense, unending little pulses continued to ripple around my cock. If she didn't stop coming...

Hell.

I didn't want it to stop – didn't want her to stop. It might kill me, the pleasure, all this craziness I felt for her raging inside me, dying to get out. But it would be one hell of a way to go.

She pulled her mouth from mine, her head falling back. The long line of her neck exposed, I bent my head and scraped the arch with my teeth and gave one final nudge of my hips. Finally, I was balls-deep inside her, she'd already come twice, and if she moved or breathed a certain way, I was going to come right there.

Gritting my teeth, I wedged a forearm under her and rolled, pulling her up on top of me.

"Oh...." The sound came out of her like a purr, and she rolled her hips against mine.

"Shit."

She smiled down at me as she placed her hands on her torso, dragging them upward. As she cupped her small breasts, I gripped her hips and arched up, although I couldn't get any deeper inside her unless I crawled into her soul.

"Again," she whispered her lashes drifting down. So was one of her hands.

I locked on the sight of that hand, heart pounding. When she reached the neat nest of curls between her thighs and started to stroke, I cursed.

"Do it again," she said, rotating her hips once more.

A flex of my buttocks had me arching up.

Her lashes lifted, and she held my eyes as she fell forward, bracing her weight on her hands. The slow, teasing pace had my dick going on red alert. Tightening my grip on her hips, I warned her. "I won't last."

"That's fine. I didn't." She bent down and bit my lip.

At the same time, she tightened those inner muscles – deliberately this time – and squeezed my cock.

"O..."

She swayed again, clenched around me again.

"Damn it!"

I surged upward, fisting a hand in her short hair and flipping us once more. Once I had her beneath me, I caught her thighs behind the knees and pushed them to her shoulders. "Take it," I said. "Take it...you feel what you do to me?"

"Adam..."

"You're breaking me, O." And that's what happened – I fell apart, coming so hard, so intensely, everything went numb. So intensely I broke.

Dimly, I was aware that she was coming too – those sweet, silken pulses that were like a hundred little caresses all up and down my cock. I heard her saying my name. Heard the low moan, then the soft weak gasps for air that slowly took over.

Afraid I'd crush her, I pulled off. Her hands caught me and held on. "Don't go," she said.

"I won't."

"Hold me...all night, okay?"

Nodding, I pulled her up against me. Another shudder went through her body.

Please don't cry...

She didn't.

Slowly, she slid into sleep.

My mind was too chaotic to let me follow.

I knew why. I was still on a hairpin trigger from everything that had happened. The adrenaline crash might have drained a lot of people, but I'd spent too much of my life riding that adrenaline edge, knowing that if I crashed before it was safe, it wouldn't just be my ass in trouble, but my whole team.

I was fine with not being able to shut down just yet.

If I slept anytime soon, I was going to see it over and over again...a weapon pointed straight toward O, and that stubborn, regal chin lifted in arrogance.

3

Olivia

"I think the worst of it is over."

Joseph Cummings, one of James's lawyers, stood in the doorway, watching as a team of make-up artists went over me. It felt like my pores were being sealed shut and the crap they'd put in my hair was the same shit they'd used last time. I'd have to wash it three times to get the feel of it out.

I hated interviews.

I hated them with the passion of a thousand fiery suns. And I just needed to suck it up and get over it, because interviews were a part of my life. Sometime soon, that would become even more the case.

That knowledge hit me like a fist, and I blinked rapidly as I thought about James.

The news was out about his illness.

I wasn't surprised, really.

It had been ten days since the ordeal – that was how I preferred to think of it, the ordeal. So much less traumatic, mentally, than that night where some self-entitled bitch thought she could have me killed so she could get closer to getting her greedy hooks into Clarion.

Both Cherise and Russel were out on bail – the power of

money and good lawyers – and both were recovering from their wounds. Both were pointing fingers at the other while looking to the remaining board members for support. They hadn't gotten any of that. Strangely enough, the *ordeal* had managed to garner me the support I hadn't been able to earn in all my years of working with James.

And that support had transferred to his son.

Reaper was currently the media darling, and he hated it as much as I hated the makeup being patted into place and the microphone and camera that awaited me.

He'd been hailed as a hero – and he was. My hero.

It could have gone either way, really, thanks to the uneasy waters he'd left behind not too long ago. But key personnel had reached out to the various media outlets and advised them of how much it would be *appreciated* if Reaper wasn't painted as a villain over a few mistakes that he'd already paid for.

The appreciation attached to my boss's name – and Clarion – carried a fair amount of weight, so I hadn't been surprised when hardly any mention was made of everything that had happened with Reaper over the past few months.

"Lips!" The makeup tech in front of me sounded way too cheerful as she announced she was ready to do the lipstick.

I'd tried to avoid this the first time I'd done a live interview, and James had calmly assured me that I would come to no harm letting a woman sparkle my face with gunk and then layer my lips with Apple Dapple Red or whatever shade they'd decided would go *so* well with my pale skin and dark hair – stunning contrasts, I'd been told.

So far, I'd worn nearly every shade of red imaginable, and a few I didn't even know were real.

And yet...I still looked like the ugly duckling, I mused, staring at my reflection after the tech stepped out from between me and the mirror. Well, perhaps not a duckling.

But I'd never grown into a swan either.

Maybe a Canadian goose.

The thought made me laugh a little, and the tech waved her hands in agitation. "Is something wrong? Should I go with a different shade of lipstick? I have a few other shades–"

"No." Shaking my head, I reached up and took off the cape, then the cap they'd used to keep my hair away from my face. "I just had an amusing thought, that's all."

"Oh. Very good." She smiled at me, and I wondered if she was new, if this might be her first job. "You look very...regal."

She looked quite pleased with herself. I imagined why. She'd come up with a way to compliment my looks without claiming I looked beautiful. That was one trait I would never own. But regal was nice.

"Regal...yeah."

The low voice sent a shiver down my spine, and I looked up to see Reaper standing in the doorway, arms crossed over his chest, a light glinting in his eyes. Something had changed between us the night of the ordeal.

I couldn't put my finger on it, and I didn't want to, but the something was there nonetheless.

He'd started coming home with me.

Over the weekend, he'd mentioned he needed to get some work done at his mother's house, and without us even discussing it, I'd packed a bag.

Bit by bit, more of his things were ending up in my place, and I'd cleared some drawer and closet space for him. He didn't say anything about that either. But I'd noticed the drawers had been filled with socks, underwear, shirts, and the like. He'd walked in on me once, holding one of his shirts to my face. The embarrassment had lasted only long enough for him to come up behind me and wrap his arms around me.

He felt it too.

Whatever this was.

He didn't want to name it any more than I did, but I knew he felt it.

Now, as I held his eyes, Reaper came toward me with a faint smile. "I'd say regal works. You look like the whole damn city ought to be bowing at your feet.".

"Oh, please." Rolling my eyes, I focused back on the mirror and smoothed a hand down my dress. It was a little more casual than I'd normally wear for an interview. Granted, this interview had been sprung on me on my way out the door, and I hadn't had time to do anything more than grab coffee, much less change.

Meeting Adam's eyes, I asked, "Are you ready?"

He lifted a shoulder as he came inside, looking around at

the equipment being set up with a wary eye. He seemed about as happy to be here as I was, but unlike me, he had no problem letting his displeasure with the whole situation show. Diplomacy was one trait he hadn't bothered to polish up on. I knew enough military men at this point in my career to know that his lack of tact would probably have hamstringed him had he stayed in the Navy much longer.

Still, I knew it burned him, having to leave the way he had.

He drew closer, and I asked in a low voice, "Will you attempt to behave this time?"

"Sure." He shrugged. "But I behaved last time. It's not my fault the media seems to enjoy being idiots. I simply pointed out that it was a dumbass question."

Indeed, he had.

The reporter in question had been present during the first press conference, and she'd asked him if he had any regrets about how things had gone down the night of the ordeal. After all, he'd helped ensure his father's sister-in-law would be facing the judicial system for her crimes.

He'd asked her if she was sure that was the question she wanted him to answer, and she'd smiled like a fox in a henhouse. It wasn't until he'd explained all the ways that things could have – likely would have – gone wrong if he and Hawk hadn't decided to take action that she realized maybe she shouldn't pull a tiger's tail.

Each time she'd tried to cut Reaper off and redirect, he'd simply kept on talking in a level, easy tone, like she didn't exist. When he finished, he'd stared her down. "I hope that answers that, but if not, I can't help you. I don't tend to put much thought into foolish questions that are meant to make the bad guys look sympathetic."

He hadn't allowed her any more questions during the interview, and she'd steamed, her eyes flicking to me, like she intended on making me pay for his poor exercise in judgment.

I guess she'd had the idea the new CEO-to-be would be easy to mow down. It was always fun, having illusions shattered.

I reached up to smooth down the collar of his shirt. So far, he was fairly resistant to wearing a tie, a fact that made little sense when I thought about it. He was former military. He'd spent enough of his life in a uniform that a suit and tie shouldn't be an issue. But maybe that was the problem. Maybe he didn't want the reminder.

"James wants us to join him for dinner at the estate tonight," I said, backing away before I gave into the urge to do a lot more than just smooth his collar down. I wanted to touch every part of him – again.

Reaper's mouth tightened slightly, but he nodded. "Okay. Why are you delivering the message instead of him?"

"He told me he'd texted you and emailed. Apparently, you're still working on catching up to the pace around here because you haven't answered him."

As we started for the seating area by the window, he shot a scowl my way. "I'm constantly getting emails and texts now. I've got three hundred ninety..." He stopped and pulled out his phone, then gave a glum sigh. "I shouldn't have looked. Now it's over four hundred. Again. How do I keep up with this? How did he?"

"That's what your administrative assistant will do. We still need to figure that out – James's admin is ready to retire." I kept it at that, not wanting to discuss how the sweet, kindhearted Mariette had all but broken into tears when James and I had spoken with her. We'd only confirmed her suspicions, but it still hadn't been easy for her to hear.

"She's still willing to stay on until we find a replacement, right?" Reaper reached up, tugging at his collar like it was going to choke him.

"Yes." Rolling my eyes, I took his hands and eased them down. "Sit. Quit fidgeting. You look nervous."

"I'm not. I'm just tired of sitting down and answering the same fifty questions all over again." He pasted a smile on his face as the newscaster in charge of the interview came rushing in and gave us a quick wave.

"I mean, how many ways can I answer the question, 'What did you think when you found out you were heir to the vast Clarion dynasty? Are you still overwhelmed?'" He managed the somber expression, the serious tone the various media personnel had used over the past week, nailing it. "You'd think one of them could come up with something new."

"Hey, at least this way there are no surprises. I don't *like* surprises from the media. It never ends well when they manage to trip you up." We settled down on the couch, leaving the chair for the anchorwoman for one of the larger news stations in the Cincinnati area.

She came our way, her eyes avid and bright.

"Thank you *so* much for agreeing to this so close to the wire," she said, settling down onto the edge of the chair. "Are you both ready? I've got some exciting questions for you."

"Absolutely." Reaper shot me a look, his brow arching incrementally.

I hid a smile as I went to take my seat. Maybe she would surprise us.

But I wasn't betting on it.

4

Reaper

"Mr. Dedman, do you have any comment? Did you, in fact, help murder those men?"

The woman's voice was like gnats buzzing in my ears. I felt like I'd been sucker-punched.

Staring at the familiar face, I heard screams all over again. Dog's. Rake's.

And her – the woman in the picture.

It was Kylie Wallace, the one and only daughter of Donald Wallace, a senator out of Georgia – the woman my team had helped rescue, only to find out that she and her mother were terrorist sympathizers who had actually been working to help fund an ugly enterprise that existed in the small town where Kylie's grandmother had been born.

I could hear her screaming...*You killed them all.*

Then Dog as he went to cut the rope, knowing that Rake was already gone. I heard his scream as he fell.

"Is what she says true, Mr. Dedman?" The newscaster continued to watch me, unblinking, while the camera rolled on. Damn, she was a persistent piece of work. "Did you kill her fiancé and his friends? Innocent men who were simply trying to take care of their village? Is it true?"

You killed them all.

The words trembled on my lips – *you're damned right I killed them all. Damn right.* But I didn't. Locking down everything I felt inside, I met her gaze coldly. "You're asking me questions about a classified operation, ma'am." My mouth felt stiff – my whole face did. Forcing anything out was almost impossible, but I had to answer. Couldn't let her think I couldn't do my job.

"You're no longer a part of the United States Navy, Chief..." she gave me a fake apologetic smile. "I'm sorry. You were dishonorably discharged. *Mr.* Dedman. You're no longer part of the Navy. Surely you can answer a *few* questions about this tragic ordeal and this woman's accusations."

"Tragic ordeal?" I could have laughed at how pitifully she'd summed up the job that had killed two of my friends. A tragic ordeal. "You want me to tell you something about that tragic ordeal?"

I leaned in, watched as she did the same. "You want to know more about that tragic ordeal, maybe you should take a good long look at your...source's political leanings and sympathies. If you were any kind of journalist at all, that would have been your first step." Narrowing my eyes, I looked at the camera. "This is live, right? There's a line for your competition to chase. The woman in the picture I was just shown is Kylie Wallace. Check out her background...look *real* hard." I looked back at the newscaster. "I'm certain her daddy will be damn happy she set you on my ass right before the election."

"Mr. Dedman–" Her eyes narrowed.

Guess she didn't like that I wasn't following her script.

Ignoring her, I rose and began to pull at the microphone I'd been wearing.

"I have just one more–"

"No, you don't," O said, cutting her off. "You were granted this exclusive on the grounds that you'd keep your focus on the events from last week and Mr. Dedman's relationship with his father. Period. Those were the details agreed to. And, for the record, Mr. Dedman was honorably discharged. I advise you get your facts straight before making a fool out of yourself."

She was still talking when I walked out of the room thirty seconds later, took the stairs immediately to my right and all but ran up the final floor to where James Clarion managed his small empire.

Those offices would be mine soon.

I was already dealing with calls from decorators to help me figure out *my style*. I wanted them all to just go away and let me put a cooler full of beer in the corner. Of course, having a beer wouldn't help anything. Because I'd want another and another.

The door opened while I was still staring down at the street. It seemed terribly far away.

When it closed softly behind my intruder, I closed my eyes. "Not a good idea, O."

"Leaving you in here to brood isn't a wise choice either."

She came up behind me and slid her arms around my waist, pressing her cheek to my back. "Who was she?"

"I already told the world her name." Closing my eyes, I tipped my head back and wondered how much hell might rain down on me for this.

"Her name, yes. But there's more to who she is, or was, than that."

Shaking my head, I said softly, "I can't. Classified. If I were still wearing my uniform, I could be facing a serious ass-kicking just over the little bit I did say. As it is now...shit. There might still be trouble."

O tightened her arms. "You won't have to handle it alone. You've got more on your side than you think."

There was a knock at the door, interrupting anything else she might have said.

We broke apart, and I turned to stare at her as the knock came again.

"Am I supposed to hide how I feel about you?" I asked bluntly.

"I..." She blinked, looking caught off-guard. "Um. I haven't thought about it."

"Come in," I called. Then I took a step forward and caught her face in my hands. "Problem solved. No need to think."

I had her mouth under mine and my tongue stroking over hers while Joseph Cummings stood in the doorway, clearing his throat. "Excuse me. I thought...well."

I lifted my head and looked over at him. "Is this a problem?"

O pushed me back and muttered under her breath, taking a few steps away.

Joseph took his time answering, giving the question the thought it deserved. "It could prove to be an issue for some. There are those who already think O seduced Mr. Clarion."

"What?!" I demanded.

"Calm down," O said, cutting Joseph off before he had a chance to respond. "I hate to be the one to tell you this, but anytime you get a woman in a position where she holds some authority, there will be those who assume she slept her way to that position."

"That's–"

"Going to be there regardless." She shrugged and moved away from me with brisk strides, clearly unaffected by the thought. "Getting upset about it changes nothing. And for the record, I'm perfectly capable of telling you what sort of problems this might present us with."

Joseph cleared his throat. "To be fair, O, you've never been in this sort of situation." He looked thoughtful as he studied her before he looked over at me. "This is a matter that requires discussion, but Mr. Dedman, you have a call."

His cell phone rang, and he pulled it out, holding up a finger as he answered. A moment later, he lowered it. "Actually, you have several calls – one says he's a former CO of yours, one is Senator Wallace, and one will not give his name."

"How about I talk to my CO – excuse me, my *former CO*." Fuck, that still burned. "You tell the others to go get fucked?"

"I'll talk to the senator," O said, resting a hand on my shoulder. "As to Mr. Anonymous...well, we prefer to have names."

"I'll deal with the third caller. I have suspicions on...well, not the exact who, but in general." He told me which line Hawk was on and while I was going to deal with that one, he connected O to the senator. I was tossing her into the frying pan here. She had no idea what was going on.

I hadn't even sat down at my desk when a small tornado erupted into the office, four suited minions who seemed to answer O's every beck and call. She scrawled a note down and passed it off. "I want it yesterday," she said as she lifted the phone to her ear and took the call from the senator.

"What in the *hell* were you thinking?" Hawk shouted in my ear.

I pulled the phone away.

"Excuse me? I can't hear you over the sound of my exploding eardrums."

"You dumbass. You're gone for a few months, and you've forgotten everything!" Hawk was snarling now. "You got any idea the kind of shit you're going to bring down on me?"

"You got any idea of the kind of shit *she* should have had brought down on her?" I demanded. "What did she end up getting? *Parole*?"

I waited.

Hawk said nothing.

"Hawk..."

"There was no trial, Reaper. Her mother has agreed to turn over information from time to time, and Kylie had her passport taken away for a few years – no more illicit trips to meet any new terrorist boyfriends."

"No..." I sucked in a breath, my head spinning. "This..."

I almost threw the phone. "I got plowed and picked a fight, and the Navy kicked me out, stripping me of the job I loved and was damn good at. Those two *sold out their country*...and nothing is going to happen to them?"

Dead silence rang on the other end of the line.

"You son of a bitch," I said, my voice low. "That piranha tries to sell me down the river and have the media burn me alive because her extremist buddies ended up dead when we everything to *save* her worthless ass. We lost two good men, and you have the nerve to call me out on the carpet because I told the media to go look in a few corners where the dirt could be exposed by anybody with eyes?"

"You have a responsibility–"

"The Navy had a responsibility to me, and they kicked me to the curb because it was just more expedient," I said, cutting him off. I was furious, still so furious. "Yeah, I went over the line, but you all could have gone to bat for me. It was my first time ever being in trouble, and it's not like I'd had the best few days."

Best few months.

"Reaper, you were already showing signs of burnout. We

couldn't take the chance that you'd lose it on a mission."

"Oh, fuck you." Maybe he was right. Maybe. I didn't know. But the Navy I'd served, the country I'd served, the life and code I tried to live by my entire life – all of it, it abandoned me when I needed it the most. And most of my friends had disappeared along with that life. "Don't you try to pin this shit on me. If you think I'm going to sit through some smear campaign that little psycho prima donna staged, you're *all* out of your mind."

"Who cares if she goes running her mouth?" Hawk snapped.

"Because it's not just *me* who gets affected now!" I wanted to hit something, but Hawk's words had hit a nerve. Maybe I had been walking too close to a line. "In case you aren't aware of what's going on in my life, I'm being handed the reins to a company that employs *thousands* and spends *billions*. You think she can smear my name and it won't affect Clarion?"

"I – fuck. Fuck you, Reaper. What the hell?" He sputtered for a few more seconds and then snarled again, "Fuck you. Shit. I gotta go and see what in the hell I can do about this shitstorm. Do me a favor and try not to make it any worse, okay?"

"Making your life hell is what I live for, don't you know that?"

He hesitated, then added, "You know you're missed, man. A lot."

"Yeah. Same goes." I disconnected and turned around to see how O was faring. Her conversation was going quite a bit smoother than mine.

"I'm afraid you can't speak to Mr. Dedman at the moment. Yes...yes, Senator Wallace, I understand you're unhappy about this, but perhaps you should be speaking to your daughter. As I understand it, she's the one who has been secretly giving money to members of ISIS." She cocked a brow and gave me a smile. "No, I'm afraid I'm not out gathering wool or blowing shit up your skirt, sir. I've actually got hard data in front of me." Another long pause. "What? Of course I have no immediate plan to go public with it. I'm certain your daughter regrets her lapse in judgment. Talking to the reporter as she did was...well, you and I both know how this can affect your chances of getting reelected. Not to mention the endorsements she gets – she has a modeling contract, doesn't she?"

Man, I adored that woman. I worshiped her.

I hadn't realized I'd taken a step toward her until she lifted a hand, shaking her head and given me a teasing, yet somehow firm smile.

"*No,*" she mouthed.

Fine. But the second she ended that call…

"Well, Senator, I'm not *implying* anything. I'm simply pointing out how unwise it was for her to have given that interview. To my understanding, Chief Dedman and his team likely risked their lives when they went into that country, and it seems to me that she…misunderstood the situation. Given her sympathies for the extremists – I'm sorry, her grandmother's family, perhaps she is simply overly emotional and…ah, yes. Of course. I believe that would be wise. Oh…by the way, as a man in your position can probably appreciate, we do receive unpleasant, sometimes even threatening calls here. I should have already informed you, but you were transferred to my secured line and all phone calls on this line are recorded. The conversation will remain private, I assure you."

A cat's smile curled her lips. "Absolutely. I understand."

She hung up a moment later and smoothed her hair back. "You can expect a phone call from Kylie Wallace within a few days. He thinks she's overwrought by the death of a man she developed an unhealthy attraction to when she visited her grandmother every summer. She also recently lost her grandmother, and she's not coping well, but he thinks that once she takes a few days to think, she'll understand."

"Uh-huh." I closed the distance and did what I'd been pondering the past few minutes as I listened to her coolly and calmly take the legs out from under one Senator Wallace.

Hooking my hand over the back of her neck, I hauled her up against me and sealed my mouth over hers.

She hummed against my lips for a brief second then opened with a sigh.

"I'm so crazy about you, I almost can't stand it." I whispered the words when I finally let her up for air and she startled me with a laugh, throwing her arms around my neck.

"That's nice. I'd hate to be the only one feeling this way."

She tipped her head and smiled up at me.

Sliding my hand up her back, I pressed my brow to hers.

The warmth of the moment faded too fast.

"How close was I?"

I didn't have to ask what she meant.

"I can't talk about it, O." Whether I was pissed off at the Navy or not, the missions I'd been on were top-secret. Even rescuing that selfish piece of work – although we hadn't really been *rescuing* her. Her daddy had sent us in to bring her back after she'd finally decided she wanted to be with her boyfriend or whatever the real story was, but she hadn't needed a rescue.

That was just the story he'd concocted to get one kickass team to go in and get his daughter.

However, as part of that kickass team and a former Navy SEAL, I was obligated to stay quiet.

I didn't feel bad about suggesting people do some looking into Kylie's background. It wasn't hard to find. I'd done some of my own over the past few months, although I'd avoided trying to find out whether or not she'd had to face any sort of consequences over the shit she'd stirred up. A part of me had already known the truth of it, I think.

"You don't have to." O leaned in and pressed her lips to my chin.

As she eased back, her amazing eyes caught and held mine. She pressed a hand to my cheek. "Whatever it was, something happened that hurt you. I see it in your eyes. And for that, I want to punch her."

"Tough girl." My chest felt tight.

She smiled widely. "Can I punch her?"

"You'd break her."

She wrinkled her nose. "Is she one of those petite, delicate little things? I've always hated petite, delicate little flowers." With a soft sigh, she added, "Probably because petite and delicate have always eluded me."

"Save me from petite and delicate. And don't ever be sorry for not being that." Sliding my hands down her back, I gripped her hips, felt the firm muscle there. "You're strong...sexy." I nuzzled her neck, scraped the arch with my teeth as her head fell to the side. "Like a goddess. An empress. If you'd lived back during the time of kings and empires, you'd have commanded armies."

A shaky laugh escaped. "Wow. Talk like that will get you..."

A knock interrupted her before she could finish.

"Whatever it will get me," I whispered against her ear. "Remember it for later."

5

Olivia

R*emember it for later.*
That hot promise was still ringing in my ears.
Two days had passed.
We hadn't had much time for later.
That knock had been a harbinger and everything that could go wrong had.
The news that I had been dreading for weeks, months...years...had finally come, and I was sitting by the side of the bed as a hospice nurse hooked up yet another bag to the IV line while Queen Elise struggled for every breath.
They'd offered to ventilate.
But neither she nor James wanted her life prolonged artificially. Elise had told me more than once that she was going to spend enough time trapped inside the prison of her body. *When the time comes, you set me free, O. Set me free and don't cry for me any longer than you have to. I'll be ready.*
I knew she was.
When you love somebody with a chronic disease that will eventually kill them, you can either develop a certain outlook

when it comes to death...or you can go crazy. There is a third option – deny the person you love the right to choose, but that's not really love, the way I see it. I knew she was ready. I'd seen it in her eyes the last time she'd drifted off to sleep.

That was a little over an hour ago.

It wouldn't be much longer.

"How is she?"

I glanced over at Reaper and lifted a shoulder. "She's dying, Adam. The same as she was earlier."

He didn't take offense at my flat statement, although I wish I could have yanked the words back the moment I said them. Being cold didn't help anything.

"Where's James?"

He'd come up behind me, moving so quietly, I hadn't realized he was there until I felt his body heat. Now, I let myself relax against him a bit and welcomed the strength of his arms as he wrapped them around my upper body.

"He went to get us some lunch."

"I could have done that. I told you I was on my way." He kissed my temple.

"I think he needed a moment away," I said softly. "Either that or he was giving me a moment with her. I don't know."

I lifted Elise's hand to my lips and kissed it. Her skin was papery thin now, even more delicate than it had been a few days ago. And she didn't so much as blink, didn't respond. It was like she was already gone and her body was just playing catch up.

Oddly enough, that thought comforted me.

I didn't want to think about the Queen, regal and proud, trapped in the prison any longer.

A soft noise at the door had us both looking over. James was there, along with one of the house attendants, wheeling in a cart. "It's comfort food time." The older man nodded at both of us. "I was in the mood for grilled cheese and tomato soup. I hope that's okay with you."

"I love grilled cheese and tomato soup." To my horror, I felt my eyes getting misty, and I had to blink a few times before I was certain nobody would see any tears when they looked at me. "The Queen would always make this for me when I had a bad day. Right up until..."

My voice faded, and I swallowed hard.

"Up until she couldn't. Then she'd have one of the ladies in the kitchen do it. And they loved you almost as much as we did," James finished.

He nodded at Reaper. "I heard you were on your way. There's plenty for all."

"I can't say I'm much for soup, but I love a good grilled cheese."

"Then you're in for a treat."

We sat there, almost like a family, using the cart as a table while we dined on homemade comfort food, accompanied by the music of a beeping IV machine.

It was almost dusk when the nurse told us it wouldn't be much longer.

At 7:02 pm, the Queen left this world for the next one, and Reaper left James and me alone for a while as we mourned.

~

"Do you love my son?"

Out of all of the questions James could have asked me, that was the one I last wanted to hear. And yet it wasn't one that should have surprised me.

We sat there, alone with Elise. Or at least the body that had once been her. He sat on one side of the bed while I sat on the other. We each held a hand. We'd been talking about small things, little memories that made us smile – and sometimes cry. We were both struggling to say goodbye.

The nurse had told us to take all the time that we needed, although that wasn't the truth.

I could take from now until the next leap year, and it wouldn't be enough.

We'd been in there ten minutes, and there were still a thousand things I wanted to say, that I wished I would have said while she was still here. Now it was too late.

And James wanted to know how I felt about Reaper?

Part of me wanted to jump up and run away. I could make excuses. Tell him that this wasn't the time. James would let me.

If I asked him, he would even let it go and never discuss it again. He was a gentleman that way. But I felt I owed him more than that.

Still holding onto Elise's cool, thin hand, I struggled for a response. "Adam is a very good man," I finally said, feeling a little lame. I didn't want to go into detail about all the things I felt when I was with him. I definitely didn't want to do it here, and not now, when my heart felt like a gaping hole in my chest. I'd managed to go most of my life without hurting like this.

Looking at James, I could see the pain behind that quiet wall of strength, and I wondered if it might be the thing to break him.

"He's...um. Well, he's a good man," I said again.

James laughed. "I know he's a good man. Just because I'm not always in his life doesn't mean I'm not aware of what's going on with him."

"What more do you want, James?" I offered him a weak smile. I *knew* what kind of man Adam Dedman was – I'd known even before I'd gone and met him at the prison. I'd known more about him than most people probably did, thanks to James.

And everything I'd known...I liked.

The things I knew about him now I loved. James wasn't wrong, but then again, he rarely was.

"Are you avoiding my question, or are you just trying to avoid thinking about it?" James asked softly.

I blushed. "Both?" I shrugged and looked away from him to Elise's thin, pale face. She'd lost so much weight over the past few months and everything that had made her who she was, it was all gone now. The pain tearing through me just might swallow me whole. I swallowed down a sob, but just barely.

"You know, it's okay if you're in love with him. And it's okay if you're not."

James's words, voiced so gently, had that sob edging ever closer. Covering my face with my hands, I braced my elbows on the bed. Wasn't it pathetic that just then, all I wanted was for the Queen to be alive so I could talk to her?

"I don't know what I should feel right now, James."

"There is no *should* on this, O. You just figure out how you feel. There isn't a right or wrong answer here...it's not a test."

I jerked my head up. "Isn't it? For fuck's sake! He's getting ready to take over a company he knows hardly *anything* about. He's a soldier, not a businessman. I'm practically your daughter, and I'll be his right hand for the first few years. You're dying. Your wife just died. Everything is a *mess. Everything*. What would the press say if they got wind of this?"

James lifted Elise's hand to his lips and kissed the back of it, gazing at her exactly the way he had the last time I'd seen them together. "Since when have you ever let complications stop you?" He didn't even look at me as he spoke. "If something is right, it's right. You don't let roadblocks stop you when it comes to being happy."

"What...like you did?" I asked waspishly.

Now he turned his head and met my eyes. "I didn't let roadblocks stop me. I let life happen. And then I lived with my actions. I don't regret any of them."

Feeling small and shallow now, I turned away. I knew he didn't. He'd loved Reaper's mother. Each time he'd mentioned her, I'd seen that love glow in his eyes. But he'd also loved Elise. It was a different love, but the two of them had loved each other in their own way. He'd never once regretted staying with her.

"I shouldn't have said that," I said softly.

"You're upset and confused. I'd rather you take it out on me than anybody else."

"Stop being so understanding." I came back to the side of the bed and stared down at the woman who'd been like my mother. She was gone. Completely gone. "We have to let her go."

"I know. And you have to figure out your answer. Unfortunately, life isn't going to wait around for you on this. It's a simple enough question...and the answer is simple too. Unless you're looking for excuses. Either you love him or you don't."

Swearing, I shoved my hands through my hair. "Not everything is black and white, James! I'm not–"

That was when I realized we were no longer alone. Slowly, dread filling me, I turned my head and looked at the door. The lights had been lowered quite some time ago. They must've been dimmed in the hall as well. Otherwise the light there would have alerted me that he had somehow opened the door without making a single sound. A handy skill for somebody in his former field to possess.

Adam Dedman stood there, not moving a muscle as he looked straight at me. He said nothing for the longest time and then looked over at James and said softly, "They're here for her, sir. Are you ready or do you need more time?"

Reaper had heard. I knew it in the pit of my stomach that he had heard – maybe he had heard all of it.

James knew as well, and he tried to offer a reassuring smile. But it fell flat. "Perhaps I need some time to myself before they come up."

Reaper gave a short nod. "I'll see to it." He turned on his heel, striding away.

I rushed after him, but when I touched his arm, he gently brushed me aside. "I need to talk with the people downstairs. They've already been waiting ten minutes."

"Adam, wait."

"You had a rough day," he said in a level tone. "Perhaps you should go get someone or something. I need to take care of this."

"Adam...wait. We need to talk."

"Not right now." He gave me a tight smile and continued on his way.

Helpless, I watched as he strode away from me, and I tried to understand just what I'd done.

I knew how I felt about him.

There was really no question.

So what had I done just now?

Aching inside, I fell back against the wall, rubbing at the pain in my chest.

6

Reaper

It was probably close to three when I finally found my bed.

Falling face down on it, I closed my eyes and told myself to go to sleep.

I could catch a combat nap and be ready to go for another day if I had to. I still hadn't lost that knack.

But just as I was drifting off, I heard the softest of sounds.

The door opening.

Clothes rustling.

O.

Once the floorboards started to shift under her weight, I rolled onto my back, about ready to sit up and tell her to leave.

I was still trying to figure out how I felt about everything I'd overheard earlier. I should have kept my ass out in the hall. It was clearly a conversation I shouldn't have overheard.

So she didn't know how she felt about me. We hadn't known each other all that long, and we hadn't spent all that much time together. The fact that I was thinking about forever had no impact on whether or not she was thinking the same thing. She needed to come to that conclusion in her own time, and logically, I knew that.

But fuck logic.

"Olivia..."

"You move like a ghost, and you've got the hearing of...well, something that hears really, really good." She straddled me in the darkness, seeking me out unerringly.

My hands went to her hips. "You need to sleep."

"I will. After this." Her mouth sought out mine.

And I felt the damp tracks on her face.

She'd been crying.

Fuck me.

How can I send her away when she's been crying?

She reached for the buttons on my shirt, her mouth moving from mine to trail a line of kisses down my jawline and neck. Letting my head fall back, I blocked out everything from earlier, told myself that all that mattered was here and now.

Then I stopped trying to pretend.

Flipping her onto her back, I sought out her face in the dim light. She was still struggling to see me, but my night sight had always been acute and years in the Navy had only strengthened it. "What is this to you?" I asked, cupping her chin and staring into her eyes.

She blinked, finally focusing on my face.

"Adam..."

I kissed her hard and fast, using my knee to nudge her thighs apart. "What is this to you?" I asked again. "Am I just a good, handy fuck, or do we have something? Are you just using me to forget about everything in your world going to hell? If so, trust me, I get it, but I need to know."

She slid her hands up my chest and cupped my face.

"Everything in my world is going to hell," she said bluntly. "Everything but you."

"That's not an answer."

"Isn't it?" She tugged me down and kissed me. "Everything inside me tells me it would be smart to keep my distance from you. This is going to complicate everything so much. I know it. You know it. But I've got a much better idea of how it will complicate things. And I just don't care." She laughed, but it was a low broken sound and just hearing it hurt. "You know, it wasn't until Elise died that everything hit me. But I've been wondering if we really should do this. I just don't know if it's smart. I want this. I want you. You're the only good thing in my life right now, but I just don't know if we should have anything more than this."

It wasn't what I wanted to hear.

But it was going to have to be good enough.

She pushed at my shirt, but I caught her hands and stretched them over her head. She tugged against my hold for a minute, but when I parted her folds and thrust a finger inside her, she forgot about breaking free and arched up against me, riding my hand and moaning.

I worked her until she was vibrating right on the knife's edge of climax and then I withdrew my fingers, lifting them to my mouth and licking them clean. She panted, staring at me. I used my index finger to trace her lips then lowered my head and followed the path with my mouth.

"No more talking tonight. No more thinking. I just want to fuck you until neither of us can think straight, until neither of us can move."

She swallowed. I heard the sound of it even if I couldn't make out how her throat moved within the dimness of the room. "Yes...yes, please."

She sounded like a school girl, trying to impress her teacher.

Catching one thigh, I pushed her leg up, hooking it over my elbow, opening her. She moaned as I passed the head of my cock up and down her slit, rocking back and forth, letting her wetness bathe me. I kept that up until she was twisting under me, her nails scoring my flesh.

"Look at me, O."

Her eyes came to mine, and as we watched each other, I sank inside her, slowly, feeling her stretch around me, the milking sensations of her pussy so sweet it almost drove me out of my mind.

Words tumbled up my throat, hovered on the tip of my tongue.

I didn't dare say them though.

Not now.

I wanted to lose myself inside her, wanted to lose myself *to* her.

Or maybe I'd already done it.

Maybe she already owned me.

She cried out my name, arching closer.

As she started to come, I thrust harder, faster.

I buried my face against her neck as I came and let myself mouth the words she wasn't ready to hear.

I love you.

∼

"I'M SORRY."

Looking up over the cup of coffee, I saw James standing in the doorway. He looked gray and tired. It seemed he'd aged five decades in the few months I'd known him.

"Sorry for what?" I wasn't about to discuss my love life with him. I'd come to respect the man and some part of me even loved the man who'd fathered me. But we didn't have a close relationship, and the cancer that was eating him alive would probably make sure we never had the time for one.

"Please don't dance around the subject." He sighed and sat down at the table across from me. "I'm too tired for it. You weren't supposed to hear any of that. But then again, I suspect you know that."

Leaning back in my chair, I studied him for a long moment. Then I shrugged. "Look, the two of us are involved on a...physical level. Maybe it's more, maybe it's not. Only time will tell, right?"

"Of course. It's purely physical." James went quiet as one of the household employees appeared and offered him breakfast. He requested coffee and oatmeal.

I declined. I'd eaten several hours ago. It was already almost noon, and I'd been making phone calls and talking with the butler, helping him with whatever arrangements I could. Most of it had already been taken care of. James and Elise were big believers in pre-planning.

But I didn't do well with sitting around. I was a man of action, always had been. Even if I was just taking phone calls and accepting condolences and flower arrangements, it was better than sitting around on my ass.

If I sat around on my ass, I'd think about O.

I'd think about how she didn't know if she was in love with me or not.

I'd think about how I wasn't ready to discuss–

"How can you not know if you love somebody?" I blurted out, glaring at James. A split second later, I realized what I'd done and shoved upright. Moving to the buffet set next to the coffee service, I shook my head. "Forget I said that. I'm just thinking out loud."

"I don't think it's a matter of not knowing if you love somebody. I think it's a matter of being afraid to admit it."

"I said I didn't want to talk about it." Pouring more coffee into my cup, I took a drink, let it feed life-breathing caffeine into my system and pretended I wasn't really thinking about what he'd said, what O had said.

"You've had love given to you easily, your whole life. Your mother was a loving woman. You had friends, girlfriends, acceptance, everywhere you went."

"And a father who abandoned me." The words escaped me as easily as they had earlier. Turning, I met his eyes. "No matter how it's painted, no matter what Mom's reasoning was, or yours, that's how it's always felt to me."

"I understand that. And you have that right. I did abandon you. Both of you." James looked away. "But you had her, and your mother loved as easily as she breathed. She loved as easily as you do."

I scowled into my coffee. "Shit."

He laughed. "There's no shame in loving easily. The men you served with, they became like your brothers, didn't they? You loved them."

Uncomfortable now, I shifted and turned away. "I don't need some armchair psych trip, James."

"No. You're comfortable in your skin. Even after the rough road you've had the past year, you're comfortable. You're confident. You know who you are. That comes with having people love you." He paused a moment. "She never had that. At least, not when it mattered the most. It wasn't until Elise and I took her in that she began to understand what it was like to have somebody love her, without condition. It took her even longer to trust that was what we had for her – unconditional love."

I looked back over my shoulder and met his eyes. "Why are you telling me this?"

"Because I know my girl, Adam. Give her time."

∼

I KNOW MY GIRL.

His words circled through my head, a nagging buzz that just wouldn't shut up. Finally, I gave in and hunted her down. It didn't take much to find her. She was exactly where I expected her to be, in the library she preferred over the stuffy office downstairs.

She had a cup of coffee that was mostly empty and a pot that was down to the dregs.

I sniffed it and put it down, making a mental note to make some more after she'd eaten. I had a feeling she hadn't bothered to even touch food.

I couldn't say I blamed her. Food was the last thing on my mind after my mom died. I just wanted to lose myself. In anything, it didn't matter. If some critical situation had blown up out of the blue, I would have been the first man ready to go.

And it would have been a mistake because my head hadn't been where it needed to be. The beauty of hindsight.

For a moment, I watched her, waiting to see when she'd notice me. She didn't, not for almost a minute.

Then her spine stiffened, and her head came up slightly, turning toward me.

I had a tray of food balanced on my left hand as I watched her turn fully around, meeting my eyes for just a second before she looked away.

"Did you need something?" she asked politely.

You could try loving me, I thought. But I kept the words behind my teeth. James had been right. She needed time. Her life had gone through almost as much upheaval as mine lately, and I wasn't someone who'd come from a lifetime of expecting rejection.

"No. I was just wondering what you're doing." A look at the desk behind her answered that easily enough. She was busy at work already, juggling details for meetings, responding to emails that were probably my responsibility and handling details for Elise's memorial service.

The funeral would be small, but that wasn't going to do as far as the memorial service went. Before her health had declined so severely, Elise had been a fairly well-known philanthropist, and people wanted to come and pay their respects.

And gawk, and eat whatever free food was provided.

The kitchen was already bustling with activity, although I suspected most of the food would be catered.

It would be a circus. Another one. And O and I had just escaped the last one.

She glanced at me as she picked up the coffee cup, sipping at what little remained before looking back at me. Her eyes didn't rest on my face any longer than a minute.

"Have you eaten?" I asked.

She shook her head. "I'm not hungry."

I put the tray of food down in front of her. "You need to eat."

She sighed and leaned back in her chair. "I'm not–"

"It doesn't matter." I cut her off. "I don't care if you're hungry. You need to eat."

She stared at me. Her eyes were cool, her face implacable. If I'd been one of her subordinates, I would have folded, no doubt about it. But I simply met her eyes and stared back.

"Just go away, Reaper," she said, sounding weary. "I've got too much stuff to get done, and I don't have time for this. I'll grab a protein bar or something later."

"A protein bar. Wasn't that what you had for dinner last night? Lunch yesterday? I'm sure you'll be a lot of good to James when you drop from exhaustion in the next few days. That's going to make him feel really good."

She whipped her head around, skewering me with her gaze. She opened her mouth, then snapped it shut. "You can be a jerk," she muttered, looking away.

Ignoring that, I held up one of the small, triangular sandwiches somebody from the kitchen had asked me to bring up. Aware she was glaring at me, I moved up to her side and put the plate down on her desk. "So, shoot me. I don't want to see the woman I love collapsing."

I hadn't planned on saying that.

But now that the words hung there between us, I realized I was glad it was said. Secrets never sat well with me.

"You..." She blinked rapidly, looking around the room like a monster hid somewhere within. "What?"

I rested my hip on the desk and shrugged.

"You heard me well enough." I reached out. She froze but didn't pull away. Brushing a dark strand of hair away from her face, I told myself to leave it at that. What I wanted was to get her naked again. Maybe keep her that way for a few hours. There was nothing like some skin on skin to make the confusion go away.

For a while at least.

"Right now," I said softly, letting my hand fall. "You're hurting. Your life has been flipped upside down. Trust me, I know how you're feeling. I'm not asking for anything from you. You don't have to do or say anything in return, and I'm not asking for any kind of response."

I bent then and kissed her.

"I love you," I said again. "Now...eat something so you don't fall over. The next few days are going to suck."

7

Olivia

The next few days are going to suck.
Man, did he have a gift for understatement.
I love you.
Why in the hell had he told me that?
I sat across from him in the limo as we made the drive to the cemetery. James sat next to me, holding my hand. None of us talked.

I wasn't sure what there was to say.

The memorial service had been so crazed, I hadn't had time to think. Last night, I'd busied myself with other small details and the same for this morning, but I knew that wouldn't last for much longer.

What was I going to do once we'd buried Elise, and I had no more reason to ignore him or hide away?

Coward.

"Elise?"

Jerking my head up, I met James's eyes and realized he'd asked me something. He'd probably said it several times, and I hadn't even noticed.

"I'm sorry. My mind is on a temporary break." I offered a weak smile and hoped he wouldn't push.

Of course, he didn't. James was too much of a gentleman to do that. "Understandable. I was saying that I planned on going to the townhouse in Cincinnati for a few days after the service." He gave me a tired smile. "It's...well, there will be ghosts at the house no matter when I go back, but I'd just as soon not face them right away. Besides, if I'm at the townhouse, it won't be so exhausting for me to come in and help Adam out a bit more than I have been."

"You don't need to be worrying about that." I frowned at him. His face was thinner than ever, more gaunt, and I saw new lines carved by grief. And he wanted to worry about work?

"It's not *worrying*," he said gently. "It's called *distraction*."

"But–"

He reached up and brushed my hair back. "There's no point in arguing. You know I don't have much time left. I love my company. My people. Let me spend my time where I'm happiest. There's nobody left at home now that Elise is gone."

Throat tight, I nodded. But I couldn't stop myself from asking, "Why do you have to be such a stubborn son of a bitch?"

"Nobody else would have been able to take you on, young lady." He pinched my chin and then settled back more comfortably in his seat, closing his eyes.

He might have drifted off to sleep.

The drive to the cemetery took almost thirty minutes on a normal day. Today, with the funeral procession, it was almost double.

Feeling Reaper's eyes on me, I shifted awkwardly and looked out the window to avoid his gaze.

"Have you slept much?" he asked softly.

"Enough." I shrugged, still staring determinedly outside.

"You didn't eat anything."

"I wasn't hungry."

"You're going to get a crick in your neck if you keep doing everything you can to avoid looking at me."

"I am–" Sighing, I turned my head and met his gaze. "What do you want?"

"You know what I want." He offered me a crooked smile, one that invited me to smile back, one that made me feel all warm and melty inside.

I didn't let myself return it, and I tried to ignore that warm, melty feeling.

He didn't let it affect him. He lifted a shoulder and stretched out his long legs. The dark material of his suit clung to muscled thighs and my belly heated as memories of feeling that body against mine rushed through me.

The way his hand felt against my face.

His eyes on mine.

My breathing hitched in my lungs, and I swallowed, jerking my head around once more to stare outside.

There's a funny thing about leather. It's hard to be completely quiet when you're sitting on it – or moving on it. I actually heard him this time, as he slid off his seat and came to sit next to me on my other side. James had indeed fallen asleep. I could hear the steady, deep sounds of his breaths, and the uneasy rattle that often plagued him of late.

Nervously, I shot Reaper a look before turning my head to resume my study of the landscape as it blurred by.

"Whatever it is you were thinking just now..." Reaper murmured, leaning in so close, I could feel the whisper of his lips brushing against my ear. "You should probably stop. We've only got about ten minutes left to go, and I'll need every last one of them if I want to climb out of here without a hard-on."

I jerked my head around and stared. Not at his face, but at his lap.

He groaned, the noise rumbling from somewhere deep in his chest, and I whipped my head up to meet his gaze. My cheeks were red, all but burning with it. He did indeed have an erection, and now, the hunger pulsing in me began to rage even harder.

"Stop it," I said half-desperately. "This isn't...we're going to Elise's funeral."

He cupped my cheek, his thumb stroking over my lower lip. "I know."

He shifted, moving to return to his seat.

I don't know who was more surprised when I reached up and caught his arm. "Wait...I mean...sit here. With me."

His eyes widened as I slid my hand down his forearm and laced my fingers with his. "Please." Licking my lips, I busied myself looking everywhere but at him. "This is…it's getting too real. Please."

"Whatever you need, O."

∼

I HATED FUNERALS.

The first one I had attended had been for Bianca, the girl who had helped Jaquan jump James.

That was a few years after James had taken me in. Jaquan had gotten the tougher sentence, and it probably turned out to be the best for him. Although it was his second time in, he was turning his life around, working with dogs and younger inmates.

He'd be out in six more months, and he planned on continuing his work with dogs, according to Demarre.

Bianca had only served nine months of her sentence, and she'd fallen in with another gang, a rougher one.

She'd been loyal to Jaquan and he to her, but she'd never been all that bright. She hadn't lasted a year with the new gang, killed by the leader's girlfriend. Jealousy ran high in situations like that, and Bianca had been beautiful. Beautiful…and stupid. Easily fooled.

I'd paid for her funeral, and James had attended it with me, standing there at my side as I tried not to cry.

The only other person to show up had been Demarre. That was how we'd met. He'd reminded me so much of Jaquan, and I'd done a double-take as fear flooded me. He'd recognized me, although he'd only been a kid when he'd seen me last.

Bianca's funeral had been closely followed by another funeral, a security guard who'd worked with James for almost as long as he'd owned the company. I'd stood with James. He hadn't bothered to hide the tears, just quietly dabbing them from his face with a pristine white handkerchief.

There had been two more funerals since then, and each one had sucked.

But none of them had been like this.

There was only a handful of people, unlike the circus that had been Elise's memorial service.

The household staff had been invited, and most of them were there. The nurses who'd cared for her in the final days were there as well. A few of her closer friends stood in a knot off to the side, weeping softly while James and the minister spoke.

I just wanted them to start the service and get it over with so I could get away from here and cry. The tears were a giant, miserable ache inside me, but I couldn't cry in front of people. I just couldn't.

The sound of a car approaching had me looking up, but it was with a casual disinterest. It wasn't until the car slowed that any of us really paid it much attention.

Even then, as it came to a stop, we all just stared.

Even when one lone occupant climbed from the back seat, none of us reacted.

Well, one of us did.

Reaper.

He stepped in front of me, the gesture oddly protective.

Cherise Sinclair looked around, her eyes huge and red-rimmed, almost wild. Immediately on her heels was a large, suit-clad man who rushed to catch up with her as she started our way.

"You thought you could keep me from her even now," Cherise said, her voice rising and falling.

"You—"

The man with Cherise caught her arm, pulling her to a stop as he held out a piece of paper. "Ms. Sinclair was granted permission to attend her sister's funeral. If you want to see the court order, it's all right here."

Lawyer. I curled my lip as I stared at the piece of paper for a second, then up at Cherise.

"Funny time for you to decide you really cared about her," I said sourly.

"I always cared!" Cherise shouted.

A few of Elise's friends fluttered their hands, murmuring to themselves, and I flushed, shame rushing through me. This wasn't the time or the place. What did it matter if Cherise was there?

Okay, she'd tried to kill me, yeah. *That* mattered.

But it wasn't like she'd try anything again. She'd have to

be crazy on top of stupid.

"I always cared," she said again, her voice wobbling.

"Cherise, if you wish to stay for the funeral, so be it. But you'll conduct yourself accordingly, or I'll have you removed," James said. His voice was thinner. He sounded weaker every day. But the threat was clear.

And I had no doubt he *could* have her removed.

For a moment, it looked like Cherise would argue.

But she must have thought better of it, lifting her chin and giving us both an icy glare. "Very well. While I despise the both of you, I'll hold it in check so I can say goodbye to my sister."

There were so many things I could have said to her.

I bit my tongue, holding all of them back.

I'd tolerate her, for now. But the second the funeral was over, she was going to get the hell away from here. Away from me, away from Reaper, away from James.

8

Reaper

I know too much about evil.

Evil can be twisted and confused...and it can convince itself that it understands love.

I was staring at the face of evil right now.

Plenty of people would think I was wrong, calling one Cherise Sinclair evil. Sure, she'd tried to arrange it so that it looked like I'd killed O. I wasn't exactly sure what her endgame had been. She wouldn't have gotten away with it, although arrogant people always assumed they wouldn't get caught. Maybe she'd just figured that if James didn't have his successor, the board would sell to one of the companies that had offered to buy Clarion before, and all the board members would be rolling in it within a few short months.

But that was just greed driving her, most people would think.

There was a difference between greed and madness and evil.

Cherise might be greedy, but she had more madness and evil in her than greed. She lived to make people miserable.

I could spot the malice in her eyes from five hundred yards.

It glinted there, an ugly little monster looking to pounce.

But she was one twisted cookie, because from time to time, she would look over at the casket where it rested, just above the vault and the rage would fade from her eyes, replaced by a misty veil of tears. After a moment or two, she'd blink those tears back and suck in a breath, square her shoulders, and the rage and malice would return.

"I think she did love her sister," I muttered as the funeral came to an end. "At least as much as she was able."

O didn't respond, her eyes drilling a hole into Cherise's face.

Cherise seemed unaware, her gaze directed solely at James.

And she was smiling.

That smile was creepy as hell.

"Come on," I murmured, curving a hand over O's shoulder and herding her closer to James. "I want to get you all out of here."

"We can't leave yet." She looked at the hand full of mourners.

"The hell you can't. We'll tell them James isn't feeling well, and you're going to tell *him* you're not feeling well."

She whipped her head around, glaring at me.

Bending my head until we were nose to nose, I glared at her. "Do it, O."

She narrowed her eyes, and I prepared myself for the argument to come.

But to my surprise, she didn't argue.

She turned on her heel and walked to James's side, tugging on his hand until he took a few steps away. As they spoke quietly, I moved over to the plain clothes officers who James had hired. They'd kept their distance for the service, but now that it was over, they were on hand and watching Cherise with unconcealed interest.

"We're going to bug out. You think one of you could maybe…stall her?"

The youngest, a tall, thin man with a scarred eyebrow, studied me. "Stall her how? You want us to arrest her? She's got a court order allowing her out of her house for the funeral, but she's expected to be back inside her home by a set time.

Interfering with that could be construed as interfering with a court order."

"Five minutes won't interfere." His partner studied me. "You think she's up to something."

"From what I've heard, she's almost always up to something." I didn't want to tell him I had a bad feeling in my gut.

He must have sensed it anyway. "Tell you what...I was only hired to hang around until the service was over...and until you three left. Once I see you all heading out, I can maybe move my car." A game smile curled his lips. "She's parked awfully close to me. I can maybe get an important call and stop in a bad place. Just for a few minutes."

"Appreciate it."

He gave me a shake of his head. "Five minutes is all you're getting, Mr. Dedman. And I'm only taking care of a call. That's all."

I gave both of them a smile and turned back just as O and James started down the path toward our car. It was on the other side of the road from where Cherise had parked, the front of the car already pointed toward the exit. From the corner of my eye, I saw Cherise throw her nose into the air and huff off.

She didn't even notice the cop as he slouched off alongside her, his seemingly lazy stride eating up the ground so that he reached his car far faster than she did. He was already pulling out before we even climbed in.

And just as Cherise's lawyer held open her door for her, the cop stopped his car. I could clearly see his phone as he lifted it to his ear.

They were trapped, pinned in between his car and a small wall of monuments. Her driver had been forced to wedge the car into that small space, and now they'd have to wait to be let out. As more cars from that lane began to back up and start their exodus, I smiled.

"You want to tell me what that was about?" James asked as I climbed into the limo.

"If I knew, I would." I shrugged restlessly. "I just had a feeling we should be...elsewhere."

Through the window O had cracked, we could hear raised voices.

I glanced over, watching as Cherise shouted at her driver to move the damn car already.

∽

I HAD a message from a Detective Michael Vogler waiting for me when I checked my phone two hours later.

We'd gone to lunch, James, O, and me. O had told me that a local ladies' club had offered to throw a wake, but she'd declined on behalf of James, explaining that he needed to limit his exposure to too many people because of his health.

I doubted that was why neither of them had wanted a wake, but I was happy all the same.

If I kept having to smile and nod at people, shaking hand after hand, while O looked like she wanted to find someplace quiet so she could cry, I might put a fist through something.

She'd fallen asleep in the limo on the way to the townhouse, but she'd woken up as soon as the car stopped.

She had a room here as well, and James had offered for her to stay the night, but she had refused.

She did accept the offer for coffee though, and we were inside the kitchen, O at the counter, staring at the coffee pot like it might make the coffee brew faster.

It wouldn't.

Ducking into the hall, I listened to the first message from Vogler.

Short and to the point.

Looking for an Adam Dedman. Call me when you get this...blah blah blah...

The second message was a bit more urgent, and it echoed in his voice.

Mr. Dedman, this is Detective Vogler with the Cincinnati Police. I need to speak with you. It's urgent.

There was another number I didn't know. Three calls. I listened to the first message with a sense of growing dread.

This is Special Agent Gail Nolan. I am attempting to reach Adam Dedman. It's very important that you call me. I need to speak with you regarding Kylie Wallace.

I ended the call and went into my phone log to find Vogler's number, tapping it the second it came up. I knew too much about Feds – a local cop might be more open. Besides, I was still pissed off at the fact that they'd fucked things with Wallace anyway.

Whatever that little troublemaker was up to, I didn't want any part of it.

He answered on the second ring. "Detective Vogler."

"This is Adam Dedman. You've been calling."

"Yes..." He sighed. "Yes, I have. First, I must ask...where are you and are you alone?"

Immediately, a chill raced up my spine. "I'm in Cincinnati." I rambled off the address. Remembering little details like that was second nature after so much time with the SEALs, although we'd gone by coordinates rather than street names. "I'm with two civilians. Why?"

"Would that be James Clarion and...ah, Olivia Darling?"

The chill turned to ice. "Why?"

9

Olivia

The moment Reaper stepped back into the kitchen, I knew something was wrong.

He was clutching the phone in a fist so tight it had gone bloodless, and his eyes skimmed the entire room as if seeing it for the first time.

"Is there a basement in this house?" he asked.

"A...what?" I stared at him, confused.

"A basement. Is there a basement?" His voice was flat.

"Yes," James responded while I was still trying to process the odd question. He was already working his way to the edge of the seat so he could stand up. His face tightened with pain, and I moved over to offer a hand. I wasn't surprised when he didn't accept it, although he did rest a hand on my shoulder to steady himself.

His breathing was far from even and for a moment, I was distracted.

It didn't last long.

Reaper caught my arm and started walking me out of the room. "You two are going into that basement. James, don't disappoint me. Tell me you have weapons in this place."

"Of course I have weapons. Now please…tell us what's going on."

He managed to deliver the words with too much dignity for a man who was breathing heavy from just walking across the living room. But the authority in his voice had Reaper stilling. Finally, he shot James a look. "Cherise didn't go home after the funeral. I just got done talking with a local cop. He's been in contact with the FBI. And the feds…well, the feds have reported that Cherise Sinclair has been in contact with Kylie Wallace."

"Kylie…" My mind blanked out on me for a minute, and I just stared at him, not following. "Who…oh. Wait a minute. That's the bitch who has been giving weapons and money to some extremists over in the Middle East, isn't it? Are you telling me that Cherise Sinclair, a member of our board of directors, is involved with a traitor?"

I was going to be sick. I knew it.

"No." Reaper shook his head. "Not on that level. It looks like she reached out after what happened at the party. She was pissed that her little welcome present to me got spoiled, so she thought she'd talk to somebody else who hated me as much as she apparently does. What can I say? People love me. Now…let's *go*."

※

"WHAT IS THIS?" Reaper asked as I escorted him into the vault.

"A safe room," James said.

I slid my hand out, looking for the light switch.

I found a light, alright – the one in my hand.

My phone had lit up. Frowning, I angled it so that the light shone on the wall. Once I had the lights on, I looked at the screen and realized I still had the phone on silent. It had been that way all day.

I didn't even remember pulling it from my purse. It was my lifeline though. I researched, double-checked, fact-checked and triple-checked everything possible on that little device.

Maybe I was thinking I'd follow up on what Reaper had

told me once we were in the safe room. When Reaper had asked about a basement, I doubted he was expecting anything like this.

I'd always assumed the place was overkill, but now I was thankful. James kept supplies down here for all the staff – clothes, food, water, enough to feed a houseful for a week. And that meant I had shoes down here. I needed to get out of these heels – they were pinching my toes something awful.

As James explained the room's purpose to Reaper, I leaned my back against the wall and kicked out of my shoes. I used the brief moment to check the texts, expecting the regular BS that came when I was out of contact.

Twenty-six texts today.

I went to shove the phone into my purse, but something made me pause.

I clicked on the little message bubble icon.

Ten missed calls.

One was from a number I didn't know, but the others...the same person who'd been texting me.

"Shit," I whispered as I scrolled through them.

It was Demarre.

And what he was telling me...

I strode over to Reaper just as he was heading back up the stairs. "You need to read this."

"I don't have time for this," he said, shaking his head.

"Make time." Shoving the phone into his hand, I turned away and looked around the safe room, searching for something specific. I found what I was looking for almost immediately and gave James an apologetic look. "I...um, I need to be in clothes other than what I'm wearing."

"I'll close my eyes, Olivia."

~

"Look, O. I can't tell ya what I don't know, and I don't know anything more than what I already said." Demarre sounded about as frustrated as I felt and maybe just as scared. "You got any idea what some of those assholes might do to me if they found out I even *called* you?"

"Yes." I blew out a breath. "Actually, I do. I...Demarre, thank you. If you ever need something, you come find me."

"Shit, white girl. What do you think you can do for me?"

It was about as much of a thank you as I could expect.

"Thank you," I said again before he hung up.

Clutching the phone, I looked up at Reaper and James. Reaper had just gotten off the phone with the cop he'd been speaking with – again – and his face was grim. "We're waiting for Detective Vogler and the FBI to ride in. Half an hour."

"That's..." I shook my head, "that's a very long time."

"Well, they're trying to get the precinct closer to come and play, but..." Reaper made a disgusted sound.

"Somebody spread a lot of money around," James said quietly. "A lot of money. I'm not sure if Cherise has access to that kind of cash."

"Kylie Wallace does." Reaper rubbed at his brow and then nodded at me. "Who was that...the kid?"

"Yes. Apparently, someone was looking for anybody interested in making some easy money. That's how it was described. This house – or the main house. Both are being watched." I swallowed nervously. "They already know we're here. I don't–"

The lights went out.

"Stay with James, O."

He sounded so calm as he thrust a flashlight into my hand.

So incredibly calm.

I reached out and rested a hand on James's shoulder, squeezing tightly. He covered my hand with his own. "Adam," he said softly. "Be careful."

"I will. You two...stay here. No matter what."

"Adam..."

I wanted to go to him, kiss him, tell him a hundred things, a thousand.

I sensed him even though I couldn't see him.

Before I knew what to say, his mouth was on mine. His tongue thrust deep, and I reached out to grab him. But he moved away. "Stay down here. Stay safe. Trust me…I got this."

10

Reaper

Trust me. Famous last words. I don't know why in the hell I said them. It was like I hadn't been able to stop myself.

Alone upstairs on the main floor of the house, I locked the door to the basement and turned to survey my surroundings. I had to give the man credit – the basement door blended in seamlessly with the wall itself. Unless somebody knew it was there, they might not see it at all.

Almost like the man had planned for a time when all things might go straight to hell.

Not that somebody running a billion-dollar arms and defense company might need a go-to-hell room.

Particularly a well-equipped one.

I had two weapons on me now, both courtesy of that go-to-hell room – the safe room as James had called it.

The CR12, fairly comparable to the M-17, was tucked under my left arm in a shoulder holster that fit surprisingly well. I had a CR-117, an automatic that was just barely toned down from the model used by law enforcement personnel in my hands. I preferred the MK 16 that I'd gotten used to on missions, but...hell, beggars can't be choosers and the weapon in my hands was one sweet piece of machinery.

I used the night scope to check out the front window, not seeing much of anything. That was fine. I didn't really expect anyone to come through the front. I took a minute to shove a heavy table against the door, turning it length-wise so that it was lodged between the door and the stairs just a few inches away. Unless somebody the size of a toddler tried to come inside, it wasn't going to happen. The table was solid oak, so good luck just busting through. It might not hold forever, but it would buy time, and that was all I needed.

I was only one man, and I only had two eyes.

The back door was the more vulnerable and easily accessible area.

That was where I needed to be.

It also was just one room away from the hall that led to the basement – and James and O.

No way was anybody getting through that kitchen.

I cleared the rooms as I started toward the back of the house, my pulse steady and slow, mind clear. Some things, I guess we don't ever leave them behind us completely.

I'd just cleared the kitchen and was about ready to settle down to wait when I heard...something.

I don't know what it was, but it was out of place.

I froze, straining to hear better and wishing like hell I had some of my old tools.

It came again. A couple of voices...and footsteps.

I brought the weapon back up and stared through the night scope.

They were in the backyard, moving up to the house.

Idiots.

They'd cut the lights almost five minutes ago.

They should have already moved in and done their job–

Not the time to be criticizing them, I told myself. I didn't *want* them doing their job well.

But seriously, what kind of dumbasses cut the lights and then hung around for five minutes? I had no idea, although I was about to find out. I adjusted the light body armor I'd found down in the safe room, making a mental note to ask him just what in the hell he thought might happen to need such a room.

The door creaked open as I settled into place by the window, staring outside.

The alarm hadn't gone off.

I stared at the screen panel and realized they'd somehow hijacked it from outside.

Okay, maybe they'd been doing something useful in those five minutes.

I'd counted six outside. There were still five, so they must have sent one in to get the lay of the land.

I'd give him a nice little welcome. The weapon I carried had a nice, sturdy strap that let me carry it around my neck. It was a little more awkward than I was used to, but I wasn't in full combat gear either. It would work though. I'd kicked my shoes off earlier – the dress shoes I'd worn to the funeral weren't exactly ideal for covert work. As the intruder came inside, I moved closer to the door, drawing the knife I'd strapped to my left thigh.

He moved far enough away from the door that I could grab him without anyone noticing.

Wrapping a forearm around him, I shoved the blade against his ribs and applied pressure. "Move and you're dead in seconds."

He moved.

I shoved the blade in. It parted his flesh like butter, and I gave it a good twist before easing him down.

Dragging him behind the door, I held still, waiting.

Someone approached, whispering his name. At least, I assumed it was his name. It sure as hell wasn't mine.

"DeLeon." A brief pause. "Damn it, DeLeon, this ain't no time to be fucking around!"

A few seconds later, a heavy pair of boots came thudding up the stairs. I got into position. Whoever this was, he wouldn't be quite so easy to catch off guard, and judging by the way the floor shuddered under his weight, he might not be as easy to take down either. A beam of light appeared on the floor, and I sensed the man's hesitation. Taking advantage, I shot my hand out, grabbed the wrist that was just barely visible and yanked.

At the same time, I slammed forward into the door as hard as I could.

A yelp of pain almost drowned out the sound of bone

cracking. Almost.

I yanked the wrist again, driving it into the door before moving out and grabbing my would-be assailant and hauling him inside. I slammed the door shut with my bare foot, then whirled the big man around, shoving him against it.

He had dropped the .45 he'd been carrying in his left hand. I kicked it out of the way, tucking the fact that he'd been toting the weapon left-handed in my head. He was a southpaw – nobody would carry a flashlight in their dominant hand and a weapon in their weaker one. I'd broken his right hand. The pain might dull his senses for a few minutes, but if he was worth anything, it wouldn't render him useless.

Shoving the blade against his throat, I waited until his eyes cleared.

It took a few seconds.

When he finally saw me, I gave him a slow smile. "You made a big mistake, my friend."

"Fuck you, boy," he said, panting.

I pressed a little harder on the knife, watched as it broke skin. Blood kissed the edge. Continuing to stare into his eyes, I smiled. "However much they're paying you...is it worth dying for?"

"Bitch, you ain't got the balls." But his eyes were wide, the whites showing all around his pupils, and sweat breaking out all over his face.

Without blinking, I pulled back on the blade, shifted my stance and then drove the blade through his shoulder. His sharp scream pierced the air.

"What were you saying about balls?"

The blade had penetrated the drywall behind him, and he was now skewered on it. Leaving the automatic in the sling affixed to the body armor, I pulled the CR12 and leveled it at him. "The safety is off. One twitch and you're dead."

Movement out the window caught my eye. Switching positions, I took aim at the door, about mid-thigh if anybody was rushing. The trajectory would send the rounds into the ground if they didn't hit anyone immediately outside the door. I didn't want any neighbors to end up as casualties. The deafening rounds served dual purposes, as I'd hoped. The men in the yard stopped their advance, and the man screaming went silent.

"You need to tell them where you are. If they start shooting, you'll be the first one hit." I smiled. "And I'm wearing body armor. Are you?"

"Don't shoot," he said, his voice barely a whisper.

"Louder."

He sucked in a breath and in a thin, but audible shout, he ordered, "Don't shoot. I'm trapped by the wall."

"Good boy. Now, you want to discuss my balls again or can we move on to more important things?"

"Take this...fucking knife out." He stared at me with hate in his eyes.

"Sure. After we establish some rules. Your men need to leave. Really leave."

"Fuck you." He reached up and closed a hand around the grip of the knife, but even that slight movement set him to moaning all over again.

I closed in on him and grabbed it, twisting. "You really want to push me?"

"I send them away, you're gonna kill me." His dark gold skin had gone pale, eyes huge. "I ain't wanting to die."

"Then you shouldn't have taken this job." I paused, glancing out the window before looking back at him. "Who's in charge? You?"

He nodded. "Those my boys out there."

I caught the knife, covering his hand with mine and tightening. He started to whimper. "And do your boys listen to you?"

"Yes...shit, fuck. Yes. Just please...stop it, okay? Stop..." He was sobbing by the time I was done.

"You tell your boys to put their weapons down and then get the hell away from them. Do that, and I'll pull this out."

He sucked in a breath and gave the order. It took a few tries to convince them he was serious, but finally, all of them had placed weapons on the ground and moved to the other side of the narrow back yard. I doubted they'd given up every weapon they had. I sure as hell wouldn't have, but with two of them down and most of their weapons gone, I'd evened the odds a bit.

"Now..." I gave him an unpleasant smile, "this is going to

hurt."

He collapsed to the floor, retching.

I wasn't surprised one of them was stupid enough to rush the door. The CR12, silencer in place, proved satisfyingly accurate as I took aim at his left leg. He went down with a scream.

"Who...what the fuck...who'd you shoot, you dumb fuck?"

Looking at the man on the ground, I said, "I'm not so sure you're in a position to be calling anybody a dumb fuck." I swiped the sweat out of my eyes as I crouched by him. "This one, I shot in the leg. I won't be so nice next time. Better let them know. You've already lost one man."

I saw the knowledge in his eyes. "DeLeon."

"Yes. Tell them."

A few seconds later, I hauled him into a sitting position against the wall beneath the window where I could keep both of him and his boys in my sight. "Tell me who sent you and what the job was."

His lips peeled back from his teeth. "Fuck."

Then he started to talk.

11

Olivia

I flinched at the sound of a weapon firing. "He knows what he's doing."

James sounded so confident.

I wish I had a tenth of his faith.

Striding back and forth across the floor, I fought the urge to stare longingly up the stairs. I also had to fight the urge to creep up the stairs and do whatever I could to help.

Reaper wouldn't need my help.

He could handle this on his own. He knew what he was doing – just like James said. But I wanted to *be* with him. Be up there, helping.

"Olivia."

I wanted to ignore James. If this was just another one of his pep talks, I thought I might scream. But when I turned back to face him, he wasn't even looking at me. "We might have a problem."

He pointed a thin finger at the array of cameras on the wall.

"It's the cops." I started to breathe out a sigh of relief, but James shook his head, reaching up to pull something out of his ear. A microphone. He'd been listening in. The cameras were equipped to pick up conversations across the street if need be, so I had no doubt he'd heard whatever it was he needed to hear.

"The cop in the rear just put in a call. And look..." he gestured to another screen, and I watched as he rewound the feed from one of the cameras in the back. One of the men crouched there had a phone to his ear.

"Now listen."

The voices were thin and tinny, but audible.

"What's going on?"

"DeLeon is missing. Now Rodrigo is in there, screaming like he's been butchered. We ain't signed up for this crazy shit, man."

"You just keep him from getting out." The call disconnected, and he shoved away from the wall, moving to catch up with the partner who was scoping out the perimeter.

"They're in on it."

"Distinct possibility." James tugged at his lower lip and then heaved himself upright. "I'm going up there."

"Like hell." I shoved down on his shoulders. He fought, but he'd gotten so weak over the past few days, his sad attempt didn't add up to much. "If I can push you around, you won't stand a chance. You barely made it down the stairs. Don't give them a hostage."

"We can't leave him alone."

"We're not." Blowing out a breath, I picked up the weapon James had laid out. I was an excellent shot – he'd made sure of it. The CR-201 was a smaller model, perfect for my hand. Checking the chamber, I eyed the stairs nervously.

"Olivia, don't."

Shaking my head, I started toward the steps.

"He has no idea. I'm not leaving him alone." I gave him a small salute and tapped the vest Reaper had insisted I put on. "Besides, I'm covered...mostly."

"It won't protect that thick skull of yours."

I gave him a quick kiss on the temple, breathing in the scent of his aftershave. "I know. But my head is *so* thick, it might be bulletproof."

The choked noise that came from him could have been a laugh or a sob. I didn't look back to check.

"You know...I never did like your sister-in-law, James," I said as I opened the door, staring out into the black maw of the basement.

"Neither did I."

I shut the door behind me. And because I knew him, I added in the code that would disable the door's opening mechanism for the next hour. If this wasn't over by then, there wasn't much Reaper or I would be able to do.

And if it was...James would be so pissed off.

I started up the steps, keeping my back pressed to the wall the way I'd seen Reaper do when he'd left. There were cameras all over the public areas of the house, a security precaution that I'd always seen as overkill. Now, though...hell, I'd give the security team a big fat kiss – each one of them – when I saw them. And I would.

The door was closed, and I stood there as long as I dared, listening before I opened it, only an inch at first, holding my breath as I prepared for an unseen attack. None of the self-defense classes I took, none of the lessons I'd learned on the street had prepared me for this sort of thing.

Finally, I decided the room immediately outside the door was empty and I slid outside.

Nobody jumped out at me from behind either hall entryway. Reaper had been in the kitchen, so I started that way, holding the pistol in a loose, two-fisted grip, guided only by the small security lights.

The first thing I heard were the weak moans and the miserable voice coming from the area near the window. I'd watched with morbid awe as Reaper had made the big mountain of a man ball like a baby. He was still on the ground, and he saw me first, his eyes going wide.

He went to say something, but Reaper caught sight of me, spinning on his heels, knees flexed as he brought the weapon up.

My heart jumped into my throat, and I stared at him, frozen.

He bared his teeth at me and stormed over. "Get back downstairs," he said. Then he grabbed me by the neck and yanked me toward him. "What were you thinking? I could have..." He groaned and slammed his mouth down over mine, kissing me desperately. The heat from his body was like a furnace, and I wanted to sink into him. I didn't have a chance to even touch him before he set me away. "Get back downstairs."

"No. There's a problem."

"I don't care. Get–"

I clapped my hand over his mouth and hurriedly told him what James had seen, what he suspected.

His eyes narrowed over my hand, and he reached up, tugging it away. He started toward the man on the ground, but even as he went to speak to him, we both heard something in the silent house.

It was incredibly, inexplicably loud – coming from the front door.

Wood banging against wood.

I'd seen how he'd barricaded the front door and in a second, I knew.

"They're trying to come in," I said, voice low.

On the floor, Rodrigo started to laugh. "That's right, you punk bitch. You ain't getting outta this. Boss is coming for your ass."

Reaper ignored him. I was tempted to smash my foot into the man but Reaper was already dragging me by the hand, hauling me toward the basement door. "Message delivered. Go be safe."

"No." I planted my feet and jerked my wrist, although all I did was make it hurt. His grip was like steel.

He turned and glared at me, eyes firing in the dark. "This isn't a game, sugar. Get downstairs."

"I know it's not a game, and there's no time–"

Another heavy thud from the front door. "Mr. Clarion. You need to remove the barricade. It's the Cincinnati Police Department. We're here to help. We heard reports of shots fired. We must come in."

From the back, there was the sound of breaking glass.

I shoved my free hand against Reaper's chest. "Go be a hero. I'll make sure nobody gets downstairs."

"I want you out of sight!"

I pointed past his shoulder. "I will be."

The library was on the opposite side of the hall, the glass

windows providing the perfect place to observe anybody walking by. Faint light from the kitchen windows reached this far down the hall, but they didn't penetrate the library. With the gloom of the shadows heavy on the house, I'd see anybody before they'd see me. More, I'd see anybody who might see the hidden basement door.

He swore and then grabbed the handle, jerking the door open and shoving me inside.

"Coming for you, punk ass bitch!" Rodrigo called out. "My boys are going to cut your balls off and make you eat them!"

"Promises, promises," he muttered as he closed the door. Through the glass, he mouthed, "Hide."

I retreated, although the only way to hide was to simply back up and let the shadows do their work. I'd have to watch for a flashlight. If anybody shined one in here, I'd be a sitting duck.

⁓

FOR THE REST of my life, I'm going to remember what played out over the next few moments.

Clutching the weapon, I kept telling myself over and over to relax. I couldn't shoot worth shit if I tensed up. I knew that. The instructors James had hired to train me had drilled that into my head.

I wanted to believe I wouldn't *have* to fire the weapon, but the hot, greasy sensation in my gut wasn't ready to think so.

When I saw the pool of light splash across the floor, I shoved myself in between two narrow bookcases, sinking my teeth into my lip to keep from crying out. The door opened, and she came inside, a young thing, dressed in a pristine uniform of dark blue, her pretty features set in a solid mask of determination. Her skin was a warm, smooth shade of brown, her hair pulled back into a neat knot. She held her light and weapon in the standard Harries method, her gun hand steady.

"Venturi."

The officer tensed, but didn't turn. "Clearing this room, detective."

"Yes. I just need to..."

I peeked one eye out from behind the bookshelf. My heart slammed up into my throat, and I opened my mouth to scream out a warning, but it never came out.

Bang!

The young officer collapsed. Shot by the detective.

"You might as well come on out, Chief Dedman. You've now killed a Cincinnati police officer. The sooner you turn yourself in, the better."

The other man turned away, not even looking around. If he had, he would have seen me, because I was too stunned to duck back into my hiding spot.

What the hell...

What the *hell*...

There was a thud from somewhere off near the kitchen and another scream. A moment later, Reaper's voice drifted to me. "Funny, but I don't recall shooting a cop. I made one of your boys into a eunuch, though. One of them is still out in the yard, clinging to his leg and crying for his mama. Two others...well, you don't want to know what I did to them. It's pretty ugly."

I made myself move.

I couldn't stay there.

If he backtracked and looked in here...

And my skin was crawling, stomach heaving as I thought about the woman lying on the floor. I knew it was hopeless, but I made myself check her pulse. Tears burned my eyes, and I blinked them away.

I didn't understand any of this. We'd called 911. Cops should have been here, and this guy had told us it would take a while – it had to be him. He had told Reaper there was somebody inside who'd taken money. Yeah, there had been. *Him*.

I don't know if he'd hacked into the phone lines or what, but he was behind this whole thing. How much money had it taken for him to agree to kill a fellow cop?

That thought brought much needed strength, and I found myself in the hall before I knew it.

I caught sight of the other cop just as he would have disappeared around the corner into the kitchen. He was big, the kind of big that made me think he'd played football in college or high school, but he hadn't kept up his physical fitness regimen, and that muscle was slowly going to fat. But he'd still be strong. Strong and fast.

"Where's the old man and the woman, Dedman? If you're a good boy, and you just turn yourself over, maybe I won't hurt them. This is all about you anyway."

"Come find me, Vogler," Reaper said. His voice had an odd, echoing quality. I had no idea where he was.

"If I have to look, you ain't going to like what happens when I find you. And if I find them first?" Vogler laughed. "Too bad I don't have time because I could have some fun with that bitch. She ain't the prettiest thing, but she's got an ass on her. Tell you what, I'll kill her first. I'm a gentleman. Her, then the old man."

"Hey!"

I don't know why I shouted at him.

He spun around, weapon lifted.

The sight of me holding a gun on him had him hesitating though.

A rush of emotions flickered across his face. He settled on severe. "You want to put that down. You're holding a weapon on a police officer, ma'am."

"Yeah. One who just killed another cop." My voice shook, but I was surprised to see that my hand was steady. "I *saw* you. I was in that library, you dumb ass."

The hand holding his weapon went white. His face went red.

The shadow emerged from the darkness like a phantom. Reaper had his pistol pointed at the man's temple before I fully realized what I was seeing. He was like a ghost. "Lower that weapon, or I'll be redecorating this place with your brains, man."

"Shoot me and she's dead." His hand shook slightly.

"No, you don't want to say that." Reaper's voice was silky. "See, that pisses me off, makes me want to rip your balls out through your throat and strangle you with them. Or worse...just beat you senseless and leave you alive so your ass can rot in jail. What happens to cops in jail, boss? Any idea?"

"You think..." Vogler laughed, trying to sound confident. "You don't think I'm going to jail, do you? I've got more protection than you can imagine. You shouldn't have pissed that girl or her daddy off."

"Oh, you're going to jail. See, you're on candid camera right now...everything you've done has been captured on film for all the world to see."

Vogler sucked in a breath and shoved away from Reaper, spinning to point his gun at him. "You fucking lying sack of shit."

"Why would I lie?"

"Get it. Delete it." The weapon wheeled back toward me. "Or I'll shoot that bitch right now."

"You won't do that, because if you do, you're dead." Reaper still hadn't moved, holding the CR12 with a steadiness that somehow calmed even me. "See, if she gets hurt, there's no place you can hide on heaven or earth that could protect you. So stop making threats against her before you *really* piss me off."

Vogler was panting now. "Fine. I'll just..." He jerked the weapon around.

I didn't see it coming.

Reaper did, and he moved, grabbing the man and disarming him with quick efficiency before the cop could point the weapon at his chin and shoot himself.

He had him on the floor, and as he started to cuff the man, Vogler began to sob and curse, the words blurring into one another. I moved forward, one hand on the wall, adrenaline crashing through me and draining out, leaving me weak-kneed.

"Is it over?" I asked softly.

"Yeah." Reaper swiped a forearm over his brow and looked around. "The idiot kids he recruited are either dead or neutralized. We just need to–"

The *click* was painfully loud.

"You fucking dick. You shot me in the *leg*." He sounded terribly young. "In the *leg*. I had somebody coming to look at me for a basketball scholarship. I was getting *out*."

He *was* young.

Terror couldn't keep me from noticing that. He sat in the doorway, covered in dirt and blood, and he pointed a weapon at us, one that shook. It was a cheap thing, some Saturday night special he'd bought for probably a hundred bucks

238

somewhere. But he was close enough that he could kill either of us – and that cheap piece of shit might or might not fire accurately.

"You fucker," he said, and his voice cracked like he might cry. "I'm going to kill you."

"No, you're not." Reaper held up a hand and took a step forward.

I saw the boy's finger tighten.

I tried to shove Reaper out of the way.

Then he was out of the way – on the floor.

Bleeding.

I screamed and lunged for him.

The boy was screaming too, crawling toward us and telling me to get away.

Then he was quiet, quiet and still.

Another weapon had fired, and the boy was holding his arm and sobbing.

James stood over us, gray in the face and leaning against the wall.

"I've called 911."

I just stared at him.

James leaned heavily against the wall. "I know the codes to override the codes. Now stop the bleeding."

Stop the bleeding...

Dazed, I looked down at Reaper. Blood was pumping from his throat. His throat.

Shit.

12

Reaper

I *love you.*
I'm sorry.
You stubborn asshole...you better not die.
I could hear her talking to me, but I couldn't find her.
I don't know why I couldn't find her. Maybe because I couldn't even open my damn eyes. If I tried to lift a hand to reach for her, my body worked against me, and I couldn't even move.
I love you. Please open your eyes.
Olivia...
I tried to say her name, make my mouth form the letters. I managed to get out *O.*
She laughed. Or at least it sounded like she did.
Her hands held mine.
Then I was lost in darkness again.

~

THAT CYCLE SEEMED to repeat itself for a lifetime. Nothing

distinguished one point in time from another, except light and dark. Sometimes I'd hear her, and I sensed light beyond my stubbornly closed eyes.

Other times, it was dark, and I hated the dark. She wasn't always there in the dark.

A couple times, I heard James.

Stubborn boy. I always knew you would be, but did you have to go and show me like this? Come on, son. Open your eyes. I want to see you again.

I thought maybe Hawk was there, but maybe I just dreamed him.

Mostly, it was O.

I love you, Reaper. Open your eyes...come back.

I wanted to tell her I was trying.

But I couldn't even open my mouth.

~

SOMETHING WAS BEEPING, and it was annoying the shit out of me.

My arm was itching too, and that was annoying as hell.

My mouth was dry, dryer than cotton.

All of those thoughts drifted through my mind, none of them really connecting. Somebody spoke in an unfamiliar voice. "Good morning, Mr. Dedman."

Automatically, I muttered, "Good morning," and I opened my eyes.

"What...why, look at you!" A woman stood at the bedside, beaming at me. Her eyes were bright green, her skin a warm gold, and she wore brightly colored clothes – the top had puppies on it. She looked ridiculous. What was she doing here?

Craning my head, I looked around, searching for a clue to that. It hit me then that I wasn't at home. Or at least not at Mom's house.

I was in the room I'd been using at the estate.

Shifting on the bed, I tried to sit up, only to realize I was partially already there.

And on a hospital bed. I went to scratch at my arm as I puzzled through things and swore as my fingers hit a sensitive spot.

"Oh, be careful...your IV site is getting infected. I was just getting ready to change it." She rushed closer.

Her words gave me a much-needed clue. A nurse.

I was at James's house, in a hospital bed and there was a nurse here.

Why...?

Memory came rushing back in an instant. Reaching out, I caught her arm. "Where's Olivia?" I swallowed, almost afraid to hear the answer. "Is she...and James...?"

A soft smile curved her lips. "She went to go eat breakfast with him, Mr. Dedman. But she's fine. I'll go let her know you're awake. You just stay put."

⁓

YOU JUST STAY PUT...

Yeah. Right.

Once she was gone, I fought with the bedrail until I had it down, then I swung my legs over the side.

I needed to take a leak. I needed clothes. I needed...

"Reaper..."

I jerked my head up at the voice.

"Olivia."

She stood in the doorway for a moment, hesitating. I started to shove upright. There. Right there. She was what I needed.

She came for me then, flinging herself into my arms and kissing me.

Fire flared along my neck when I went to pull away, and I swore, lifting a hand to the area. I encountered a thick pad of bandages.

She eased away, staring down at me. I must have looked confused because she touched her fingers to my hand. "He shot you. The kid. Right in the neck. A centimeter to the left, and I wouldn't have been able to keep you from bleeding to death. And if James hadn't already called for an ambulance...you almost died. You had to have three transfusions."

Her face crumpled like she was going to cry.

"Don't." Tugging her to me, I held on tight. "I'm here. Okay? I'm not going anywhere."

"You better not. Stubborn bastard." She kissed me again, raining soft little caresses all over my face. "You were asleep for two days. *Two* days. You scared me to death."

I pinched her ass. "Serves you right. Know what it did to me when I saw you in the hall?"

"I couldn't stay down there. I couldn't...the cop." She swallowed, shuddering in my arms. "Vogler was dirty. He had two people, one in dispatch and another at the local precinct. They had it all planned out. There might even be more. The FBI is investigating Kylie now. She won't geting off so easily this time."

I grimaced. "Yeah, right."

She touched my cheek, tears burning her eyes. "You're awake. I'm almost afraid to really believe it's real."

I managed a smile. "Hey, I'm a SEAL." I stopped, almost corrected myself. I *was* a SEAL – former. But then I stopped. The bitterness that would have driven that was gone, completely gone. Yeah, I wasn't getting that old life back, but this new one...well, it didn't totally suck. And once I made Olivia fall in love with me...

I love you.

Wake up...

"Wait a minute." I slid a hand up her back and closed it over her neck. "You've been here. Talking to me, haven't you?"

She nodded, curling her arms around my shoulders.

"She barely left your side."

I looked to the doorway. I did a double take when I saw James was in a wheelchair. He looked like he'd aged a decade, down to nothing but a shadow of himself. But he was smiling.

O snuggled in closer, her hand fisting in the loose t-shirt I wore. "Figures you'd wake up when I left to shower and eat. Jerk."

"Hey...be nice." Covering her hand with mine, I stared into her eyes. "I heard you talking to me."

"Did you?" A faint smile came and went. "I hoped you would. It's supposed to...what? What's that look for?"

Intently, I reached up, cupping her chin. "You said something. Did you mean it?"

"Oh." She licked her lips, her cheeks flushing red. "Um...yeah. Yeah, I meant it."

James cleared his throat from the doorway, but I didn't look away from her.

"Then tell me now."

Her face softened. "I love you, Reaper. You stubborn bastard."

"Hot damn." I kissed her then, ignoring the man in the doorway watching us. He cleared his throat again, and after a minute, I looked at him. "Look, Dad...I'm in the middle of kissing my woman, can't this wait?"

A brilliant smile lit his face.

"It can." He coughed then and started to back out. "I'll just...go finish my breakfast. Your...um...your doctor is on his way in. Soon."

I nodded, but my attention was already back on O. "Say it again."

"I love you, Adam Dedman."

Pressing my brow to hers, I said softly, "Olivia Darling...I love you."

13

Reaper

It was a sunny day when we buried my father. O and I stood together feeling the heat pounding down on us while the scent of what seemed like a thousand roses perfumed the air.

Everybody else had left, save for those who were waiting to lower James Clarion's casket into the ground.

O held onto one of the roses. A diamond ring sparkled on the same hand that held the rose. James had been watching when I asked her to marry me, and a day later, he'd given away the bride. Granted, it had all happened in his room at the estate, because he'd been too sick for anything else by that point.

"We should go," she said quietly.

"I know." I slid my hand down and took my wife's hand, squeezed gently. "Are you okay?"

"Sure. I'm great." She gave a watery laugh. "We should go."

"Where do you want to go?"

"I don't know." She sounded a little lost.

"I have an idea." Tugging her hand until she faced me, I

leaned in and pressed a kiss to her mouth. "You might not like it…but…do you trust me?"

"Absolutely." She smiled against my lips. "I love you."

⁓

"I LOVE YOU. But absolutely *not*." She hissed the words at me, keeping her voice low so the kid in the bed a few feet down the hall wouldn't hear.

"James would like it." I knew it in my gut.

She crossed her arms over her chest and glared at me. "That boy *shot* you. I almost *lost* you because of him. He should be in jail."

"He would be…if James hadn't intervened. The kid has never had a break in his life. Kind of sounds like somebody else I know." I arched a brow at her and cocked my head.

She opened her mouth to argue. I thought she might be done when a few seconds of silence passed, but then she jabbed me in the chest with her finger. "I never *shot* James. Or anybody else for that matter."

"But if he hadn't pulled you out, what would have happened? You don't know." I lifted a shoulder. "You were given a chance. Now I want to give him one. Of course, if he acts like a punk ass kid…"

She closed her eyes. "You're serious about this."

"Do you think James would have done it?"

After a moment, O nodded. "He would have. And I would have yelled at him too."

She walked past me and peeked inside the room.

The kid inside, Antonio Juarez, was staring out the window despondently. His leg had been shattered when I shot him, and he had a number of surgeries ahead of him. He hadn't been lying. He'd had a promising career ahead of him. I didn't feel bad about pulling the trigger, not really. He'd also had a promising life of crime ahead of him. I knew it wasn't easy staying off the streets, but others had done it.

Still, if I could give him a chance, like James had given O…

I moved to stand with her, reaching for her hand.

"He would like it," she said, her voice so low, I barely

heard her. "Okay."

I smiled down at her and then we stepped inside.

He finally turned his head to look at us, his gaze flicking disinterestedly over our faces before he went back to staring outside. "Go the fuck away. I ain't want to talk to no reporters," he said sourly. "I don't care what kind of money you want to pay."

"I'm not a reporter, Antonio."

He stiffened. Slowly, he turned his head and looked at me, eyes going wide. "You. What the fuck do you want?"

I grabbed a chair and pulled it closer, gesturing for O to sit. Then I pulled the other over. "Tell me something...if you'd had another choice besides running with Rodrigo, would you have taken it?"

"Just get the fuck out of here, man." He jutted his chin toward the door. "I don't wanna talk to you."

His eyes flickered over the stitched up scar on my neck, though. Lingering. His face flushed, and he hurriedly looked away.

"Don't you like seeing your handiwork?" I asked.

"You want to see yours?" he demanded belligerently. As he went to jerk the blanket off his leg, I caught his wrist.

"I don't care if you show me or not. But keep in mind – I had six men and a dirty cop coming for my ass. You think I'm going to feel bad that I protected myself, the woman I love, and my father?"

Defiance glinted in his eyes as he glared at me. "Gotta be nice, having people, I guess. I might have done the same thing. Hell, I did. Why you think I was running with Rodrigo anyway? He *was* my family."

"You weren't related."

"It don't matter. He was all I had." He shook his head. "Now he's gone. My scholarship is gone, my *leg* is practically gone. I got *nothing*."

"You've got brains." Leaning forward, I met his eyes. "Tell me something...if you had a second chance, would you take it?"

"Man, just leave me alone, okay?" His eyes tracked to O before he looked back at me and flipped me off. "I ain't in the mood for your mind games."

"They aren't games." O caught his gaze. "I was you once."

"Whatever."

She smiled at him. "I want to tell you a story."

And she started to talk.

Antonio, despite himself, started to listen.

I leaned back in my chair, content to do the same.

Later, as we left, O looked at me and smiled. "James would have liked him."

I kissed her.

"I still don't," she said when I let her go.

"You will."

She laughed and wrapped her arms around me. "I love you."

"Don't ever stop."

~The End~

Also By Shiloh Walker

Sign up for Shiloh's newsletter and have a chance to win a monthly giveaway.

Look for Shiloh's Latest…

Ruined

One of the Barnes brothers, Sebastien has always felt blessed. Not only does he have an amazing family, but he's become a Hollywood golden boy who has everything he's ever wanted—with one exception. He's had a thing for Marin since he was a kid, but when he finally summons the courage to ask her out, she turns him down. Marin is ready to settle down, she wants commitment and stability, and Sebastien is still too much of a playboy, caught up in the wild life of the spotlight.

Still reeling from the rejection, Sebastien's luck runs out later that night when he saves a girl from an assault. The shining knight role fits him just fine, but his armor—and his perfect life—become tarnished when the near-deadly attack lands him in the hospital. Physically scarred, he gives up acting and retreats from everybody.

If anyone can pull Sebastien back from the abyss, it's Marin. But first she has to convince him that beauty is *not* only skin deep…

Also by M. S. Parker

The Billionaire's Mistress
Con Man Box Set
HERO Box Set
A Legal Affair Box Set
The Client
Indecent Encounter
Dom X Box Set
Unlawful Attraction Box Set
Chasing Perfection Box Set
Blindfold Box Set
Club Prive Box Set
The Pleasure Series Box Set
Exotic Desires Box Set
Pure Lust Box Set
Casual Encounter Box Set
Sinful Desires Box Set
Twisted Affair Box Set
Serving HIM Box Set

About Shiloh Walker

Shiloh Walker has been writing since she was a kid. She fell in love with vampires with the book Bunnicula and has worked her way up to the more...ah...serious works of fiction. Once upon a time she worked as a nurse, but now she writes full time and lives with her family in the Midwest. She writes romantic suspense and contemporary romance, and urban fantasy under her penname, J.C. Daniels. You can find her at Twitter or Facebook. Read more about her work at her website. Sign up for her newsletter and have a chance to win a monthly giveaway.

About M. S. Parker

M. S. Parker is a USA Today Bestselling author and the author of the Erotic Romance series, Club Privè and Chasing Perfection.

Living in Las Vegas, she enjoys sitting by the pool with her laptop writing on her next spicy romance.

Growing up all she wanted to be was a dancer, actor or author. So far only the latter has come true but M. S. Parker hasn't retired her dancing shoes just yet. She is still waiting for the call for her to appear on Dancing With The Stars.

When M. S. isn't writing, she can usually be found reading– oops, scratch that! She is always writing.

Printed in Great Britain
by Amazon